Timothy Young

N. VIAU

Just
One
Thing!

Drawings by Timothy Young

Schiffer Publishing Ltd

4880 Lower Valley Road • Atglen, PA 19310

Other Schiffer Books on Related Subjects:
The President and Me: George Washington and the Magic Hat, Deborah Kalb,
ISBN 978-0-7643-5110-5
Grandfather's Secret, Lois Szymanski, ISBN 978-0-7643-3535-8
Leonard Calvert and the Maryland Adventure, Ann Jensen, ISBN 978-0-7643-3685-0

Type set in Oopsy daisy/Mom's Typewriter/Eplica

ISBN: 978-0-7643-5162-4
Printed in China

Published by Schiffer Publishing, Ltd.
4880 Lower Valley Road
Atglen, PA 19310
Phone: (610) 593-1777; Fax: (610) 593-2002
E-mail: Info@schifferbooks.com
Web: www.schifferbooks.com

For our complete selection of fine books on this and related subjects, please visit our website at www.schifferbooks.com. You may also write for a free catalog.

Schiffer Publishing's titles are available at special discounts for bulk purchases for sales promotions or premiums. Special editions, including personalized covers, corporate imprints, and excerpts, can be created in large quantities for special needs. For more information, contact the publisher.

We are always looking for people to write books on new and related subjects. If you have an idea for a book, please contact us at proposals@schifferbooks.com.

For Rick, Greg, and Paul

Contents

Acknowledgments

Thank you to Pete Schiffer, Cheryl Weber, and the entire team at Schiffer Publishing, and to Timothy Young, the super-talented illustrator who brought Ant's drawings to life.

I am beyond grateful for the encouragement and support I've found through SCBWI, my critique groups, the KidLit Authors Club, and all authors I've had the privilege of meeting in person and via social media.

A heartfelt thanks to my sons, daughters, and grandkiddos whose adventures inspire me, and to the neighborhood "Loons," my flock of supportive friends.

Finally, a big thank you to my husband Paul, a man who knows the right time to offer a word of encouragement, and the best time to be quiet. Without you, I would've quit a long time ago.

CHAPTER ONE

THE CLOUD OF DOOM

I didn't mind being Anthony Calvin Pantaloni for the first eight years of my life, but then—**KA-BOOM!** While calling roll, my third-grade teacher, Mrs. Argyle, squeaked out, "Anthony Calvin *Panty* Loni?"

Panty? What?! In that exact minute, a big, fat, dark **Cloud of Doom** started forming over my head. I shrunk under my cloud, hoping for invisibility.

One kid asked, "Panty, who?"

Another answered, "Panty Loni?"

Before the rest of the class caught on, I blurted out, "I'm Anthony Calvin *Pantaloni.*" Mrs. Argyle nodded and moved on to her next victim. Thankfully, I was able to complete five whole months at Parish Elementary without anybody comparing me to underwear.

But that stupid **Cloud of Doom** never went away. Instead, it grew . . . and grew. And GREW! Mom and Dad got divorced; Dad moved out of Philly, and I moved in with Dad. I don't remember much about the end of third grade in my new school. Dad tried his best to bust me out of my gloomy mood, but he couldn't. I was a pretty miserable excuse for a kid.

Things got better in fourth grade. Not only did my teacher Mr. Vanichek get my name right, he believed in something called "active learning." He had us do Random Bits of Activeness every other day. On R. B. A. days, we painted ceiling tiles in the library, made sculptures out of stuff we found on nature walks, and played math games. No one bullied anyone. No one stuck whoopee cushions on chairs. No one left boogies under their desks. I fit in. I settled in. I settled into life without Mom, too, and the **Cloud of Doom** completely disappeared.

It came back today.

CHAPTER TWO
KA-BooM!

"Ant, let me see your answer to number five?"

Marcus is attempting to cheat on the Fifth Grade Math Assessment classwork. He's my best friend and I should let him copy my answer, but I don't. "Use twelve as the common denominator," I whisper.

Marcus Goldman moved into my neighborhood over the summer. He's the only one who calls me Ant instead of Anthony. Ant is a good name, a cool guy's name. I'm starting off my last year at Carpenter Elementary on the right foot.

I hand in my paper and watch the clock. **TICK, TOCK. TICK, TOCK.** Fifty minutes and thirty-two seconds until lunch. I try to read over the classroom rules Mrs. Merryweather has posted on the board, but I can't concentrate. My favorite sandwich—tunafish and pickles on a hot dog bun—is calling to me from my locker at the back of our classroom. I swear I can smell it. My stomach makes a loud noise— **GRrrRURT!** I cough to cover up the noise. I can't have anybody mistaking my growl for a muffled fart. Marcus let a fart loose on the bus this morning and some kid called him Marcus Fartcus. Fifth-grade kids will find one thing—good or bad—to hold over your head, and unless you're like Marcus and a foot taller than everybody, you have a pretty good chance of carrying that one thing with you all the way to middle school.

My stomach decides it's R. B. A. time and starts sending messages to my legs: *Alert! Alert! Get the tuna!* My feet twitch. I inch to the edge of my seat. The second the noon bell rings, I jump up.

"Mr. Anthony C. Pantaloni," Mrs. Merryweather snaps. "I have not dismissed you." Mrs. Merryweather taps her silver baton—the one leftover from her glory days as a high school twirler—on Classroom Rule Number Three:

3. NO STUDENT SHOULD LEAVE HIS OR HER SEAT UNTIL FORMALLY DISMISSED.

"Ant, sit down," Marcus says. Marcus has the voice of a bullfrog. Cory Bennett, a.k.a. the kid who's been held back twice, shoots us an evil look.

"What's the matter, Ant C. Pantaloni?" Cory asks. "You got ants in your pants? Huh, Ant C. Pants? Antsy Pants! Antsy Pants!"

KA-BOOM!

Hello, **Cloud of Doom.**

I slink into my math notebook, grab my Star Wars pencil, and push it across the paper. I have to do something—something that will make it seem like I don't care about being called Antsy Pants. The doodle starts out as a few lines, sort of like connecting rectangles. It grows into a spider web and soon takes over the entire top left corner of a page.

Mrs. Merryweather yaks away, giving us a mini lecture on name-calling. Her whiny voice shoots chills through me like fingernails on a chalkboard.

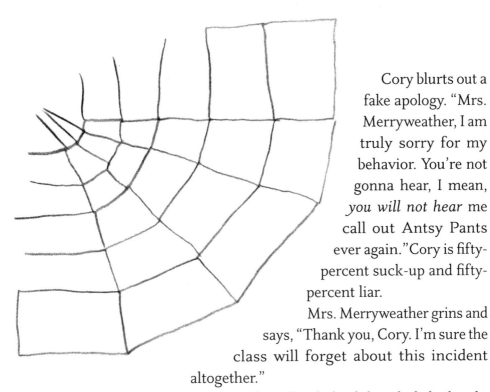

Cory blurts out a fake apology. "Mrs. Merryweather, I am truly sorry for my behavior. You're not gonna hear, I mean, *you will not hear* me call out Antsy Pants ever again." Cory is fifty-percent suck-up and fifty-percent liar.

Mrs. Merryweather grins and says, "Thank you, Cory. I'm sure the class will forget about this incident altogether."

A kid can hope. After all, I dodged the whole bad nickname thing in third grade. But fifth-graders are brutal, and I've got a bad feeling. Antsy Pants will stick to me like gum on a hot summer sidewalk.

Mrs. Merryweather dismisses us for lunch, row by row. My row is last, and I get up to leave.

Mrs. Merryweather clears her throat. "Anthony, since you need to practice staying in your seat, you will remain here until the entire class leaves. Then you may join your friends for lunch in the cafeteria. Use this time to review the rules, please."

I plop down and watch the kids file out. Cory turns and mouths, "Antsy Pants. Antsy Pants." Mrs. Merryweather doesn't see. She doesn't see the other six kids who do the same. Or the two at the end of the line who are flinging spitballs into the curly-haired girl in front of them. I ignore them all and dive into my spider web doodle.

I draw a long line down the left margin, and add a hairy spider with big Jersey hair and a baton. I write "Mrs. Merryweather" on the baton.

Then I stick a teeny Cory in the web and put the words "HELP ME !" in a balloon. In the right margin, I draw a ginormous, tattooed Principal Paulson holding a can of Spider-Be-Gone spray.

For the next half-hour, my hand flies across the page as I put in a few funny details: a Harley for the principal, a rainfall of tears streaming down Cory's pimpled face, and fat lips, crooked teeth, and army combat boots on the Mrs. Merryweather spider.

Before I know it, everybody's back from lunch. I realize three things. One, drawing keeps me busy. Busy enough to almost forget my new nickname. Two, when I'm busy, I'm not antsy. And three, my stomach is making those farty noises again. GRrrRURT! I should've eaten the tuna.

My DOODLES

Please doodle here if this is YOUR
copy of *Just One Thing!*

CHAPTER THREE
NOT THE *WRITE* PRESENT!

I do not have attention deficit disorder. I know because I was tested for it. Twice. The docs say my problem is that I get bored easily. I'm in a hurry to get to what happens next. And today, lunch was next! If only I could go back in time and start the day over.

The last hours of school are pretty busy. We get books, handouts, and homework assignments. Nobody calls me Antsy Pants. And that's huge. Maybe this one thing won't get attached to me. Maybe I'll get lucky. Maybe the kids will forget about it. Maybe Marcus will learn fractions. Maybe the moon will start revolving around the sun.

Mrs. Merryweather dismisses the walkers first, and I take off down the sidewalk. My house, which is not really a house—it's a barn—is less than a mile from school. Dad bought it cheap when we moved from our South Philly neighborhood to here: Piperville, New Jersey. Our place sits on this two-acre lot that used to be part of a large farm, but the farm got sold off and now three-story houses form a circle around us. If I spin really fast, the houses blur into one gray fence. The blur is called Sandpiper Reserve. There's not a sandpiper in sight.

Our barn sticks out like an old country store stuck in the middle of a bunch of skyscrapers. Dad's slowly making it look more house-like and less barn-like. He's a terrific architect. Slow, but terrific. With any luck we'll have closets and doors by Christmas. I don't mind hanging my clothes from the rafters, but I miss having a bathroom door. Sometimes a sheet on a pulley just isn't enough.

Even though it's not perfect, I like living in a barn. Our Philly row home was narrow and cramped. It had windows, but only in the front and back. And the whole place stank of sauerkraut and garlic. The Pfluegers, who lived next to us on the  left, cooked German food every night. And the Matuccis to the right drowned everything in garlic.

The one good thing about that row home was that it came with a mom. Mom lives in France now. She went to Paris for a vacation and never came back. I have a hard time imagining Mom living there. I have a harder time imagining her here in a big old barn.

My bedroom is where a hayloft used to be. It has a fresh smell, maybe even a real hay smell. It's a cross between a pine tree and dish detergent, and it reminds me of a clean hamster cage. My cousin, Ella Wendy, has the hayloft next to mine. Her parents, Aunt Loretta and Uncle Ralph, are in the army. They got shipped overseas at the beginning of the summer. That's when Ella Wendy came to stay with us. And that's when I started wishing she was an eleven-year-old boy instead of a fourteen-year-old girl. Dad's constantly reminding me to be nice to Ella Wendy and to make her feel like she fits in. He says, "Put down the toilet seat. Try not to snore. Don't leave dirty dishes in the sink." I want to know what Elwen—she hates it when I call her that—will do to fit in. So far, she's no different from the loud, helpless, spoiled brat I've known my whole life.

I slide open the barn door, our front door. Ella Wendy's weird music hits my ears. "Yo, Dad, I'm home," I yell.

"Hi there, fifth-grader!" Dad says cheerfully. "How was your first day?"

I slump into a nearby chair. "I got Mrs. Merryweather for a teacher."

Dad chuckles. "Benita Merryweather?"

"Think so, why?"

"I had a professor in college by that name. At St. Joe's. She was a nun then."

"If it's the same person," I say, "she's now a baton-twirling elementary school teacher."

"Oh, no! She still carries that baton?"

"Yep."

Dad and I both crack up.

"Anything else new this year?" Dad asks.

"Nope." Dad doesn't need to hear that his son's name has been butchered into Antsy Pants. I change the subject. "What's Ella Wendy listening to?"

"*Hits of Broadway,* Volume I. I think we need to prepare ourselves for Volumes II and III. Tomorrow she's auditioning for the Piper Players. It's a community theater group. They're doing a musical this fall."

"Seriously?"

Dad nods and turns his attention to the blueprints on his slanted desk. Ella Wendy has turned off her stereo, but now she's practicing lines from some old movie. She can't make up her mind how to say them: "*Could* you guys excuse us for a few minutes?" or "Could *you guys* excuse us for a few minutes?" or "Could you guys *excuse* us for a few minutes?"

"You're excused!" I yell up to her. I turn to Dad. "It was way better when it was just the two of us."

"It's temporary," Dad says. "Hey, a package came for you today. It's in the kitchen."

"Really?" I ask. "Who's it from?"

Dad gives me the concerned-father look. "Not your mother," he answers. "Don't get your hopes up."

I shrug a shoulder and pretend I don't care. I used to get a phone call once or twice a month, and a card or present every few months. Lately, Mom's been sending shorter and shorter emails with bigger and bigger pictures of famous tourist attractions like the Eiffel Tower and Notre Dame.

I get up, walk to the corner of our barn, and spy a medium-sized package on the table. The return address says Florida, so right away I know it's from Uncle Dave. I have a feeling it's a birthday present because I get one from him every September. My birthday is in March, but that doesn't matter. Uncle Dave sends the absolute best gifts ever. For my last birthday I got a set of four 3-D dinosaur puzzles from the National Science Center. I thought they'd be hard to put together, but it only took me an hour to do them. Now, when I have nothing to do, I take them apart, mix the sets up, and make up my own dinosaur. I made a carnivorous Antapooptisauropus last Tuesday. I put Stegosaurus scales in his gut, and when I pull his left arm, puzzle poop comes out. Totally awesome.

I crack my knuckles and peel away the orange and blue striped wrapping. As I'm tearing it to shreds, I remember how Ella Wendy treats presents. She opens every one so slowly that fungus could grow in the time it takes her to get to the good stuff. She even saves the paper.

My "good stuff" is a rectangular cardboard box with strange writing on it:

The Art of Calligraphy

What? Inside the box is a thin pen with two different bottoms. There's a bottle of black ink and a bottle of blue ink. They look as if they're from the pioneer days. There's also a roll of crispy paper and a guide: *How to Do Calligraphy*. The guide has samples of fancy letters, plus loads of instructions (in French, German, Italian, and Chinese!) explaining how to make those letters using the pen. I already know how to write the alphabet. Regular and in cursive. Who needs calligra-whatever? What was Uncle Dave thinking? Where is my cool gift? I put every part of the calligraphy set back into the box and stare at it. Hmm, Ella Wendy has a birthday soon. What if I rewrap this and give it to her? Dad says regifting is when you take a present you don't want and you give it to somebody else. Then you don't waste time, energy, and money buying a new one. Plus, I'm supposed to be nice to Ella Wendy. I can regift this set to my cousin. Perfect.

I scoop up the wrapping paper pieces that have dropped on the floor—there are about twenty of them—and duct-tape them around the box. It's hard to line up the jagged stripes so they're straight, but I do a decent job. Besides, it's a thought-that-counts kind of present. It's also an I-don't-want-it present, but Ella Wendy doesn't know that.

I put the box in the middle of the kitchen table. It looks like it's never been opened. Okay, so not really.

While I wait for Ella Wendy, I open the fridge and pick at some leftover fried chicken, mashed potatoes, and Boston cream pie. Then I top off my snack with some milk straight from the carton.

From the other side of the kitchen I hear, "Don't do that. It's gross."

I take another swig, and let loose a milky burp. URP!

"You're disgusting," Ella Wendy says.

I burp again just because I can. "Your acting is disgusting." I shove my butt into the fridge door and it swings shut.

Ella Wendy brings her nose close to mine and goes into drama mode. "Get used to it because I need to practice my acting, and my singing and dancing." She twirls around the table. "My audition is everything to me. I need to be fantastic! The drama teacher is straight from New York City." Ella Wendy throws her hands up, then bows, like she's waiting for an audience to applause.

I burp out three words. "Get *URP.* Over *URP.* Yourself *URP.*" I wipe the milk snot on the sleeve of my hoodie.

"Pig." Ella Wendy sighs.

"I can burp the alphabet, too. A-*URP.* B-*URP.* C-*URRRP.*"

Ella Wendy puts her palm up like a traffic cop. "Stop! It! I do not want to hear this." She shakes her head so hard her black hair flaps against her cheeks. Then she slides her shrimpy body into a chair and asks, "What's with the present? Did you run over it with the tractor?"

"That's your birthday present, Elwen," I tell her. "From me. It's better on the inside."

"Don't call me Elwen. It's not appropriate for an actress." Ella Wendy makes her eyelids into slits. "My birthday isn't for two more weeks. Is this a joke? Like what you did to me when I visited last Christmas Eve? I don't want to repeat the toy rattlesnake disaster." Ella Wendy pokes the present with her finger, then pulls it back fast. "Will anything jump out?"

"You were the disaster," I remind Ella Wendy. "You fainted into the tree and the tree smashed into the dinner table."

"It's not like I did that on purpose," Ella Wendy says. "So?"

"So, nope," I answer. "Nothing will jump out. Promise."

Ella Wendy starts to unwrap the present. Too slowly. Too carefully. She takes forever! I pull a napkin out of the napkin holder, grab a pen, and doodle. I start by tracing the puffy flower design, and then turn the flower into a Christmas tree. Next, I add Ella Wendy freaking out over the snake-in-the-box and Dad racing to the rescue.

Ella Wendy finally gets the paper off. She opens the box and stares at what's inside. She doesn't say a word. I'm not even sure she's breathing. She's frozen. Like a brain-dead zombie.

I twirl my pen between my fingers. "Check out the *How To* guide," I say, pushing the mini book in front of her. Part of me doesn't care what my cousin thinks about this dumb gift. Then there's this part that does. It's this last part that makes me say, "If you practice, you can learn how to make swirly letters."

Ella Wendy inches her chair closer to mine. I get ready for a solid punch in the arm because that's what she does at least once a day. She's been doing that to me for no good reason ever since I can remember. But what I get instead is a hug—a big, fat, gushy, girl hug. Yuck.

I keep my arms super-glued to my side. Pantaloni men are not huggers. I come from a long line of non-huggers. "What are you doing?" I ask, squeezing out of my cousin's grip.

"Thanking you, you moron," Ella Wendy whispers. Her eyes are wet in the corners.

"Why are you crying? It's just some stupid art set."

Ella Wendy shrugs. "Anthony. Dear, sweet, clueless Anthony," she says taking a deep breath as if preparing to sing the national anthem at the Phillies game. "Before my mom left for the Middle East, she took a class in calligraphy. When she writes to me, she signs her name using these fancy letters. I've always wanted to be able to sign mine like that, and now . . . now I can."

Is Ella Wendy acting? Is she testing me? I've never seen this side of her before, that's for sure. Maybe she's not a self-centered brat all the time. And maybe it won't be so hard to be nice to her some of the time.

CHAPTER FOUR
CHICKEN FIGHT

I climb the ladder to my loft, unzip my backpack, and dump out the first-day-of-school junk. Dad has a bunch of forms to fill out. I have homework—twenty math problems. Review stuff. Cake. I flip open my book and in less than five minutes, I've figured out each answer without writing down a single number. Trouble is, Mrs. Merryweather wants homework in writing, in our math notebook. Her list of rules is tattooed on my brain. Classroom Rule Number Eleven:

11: ALL HOMEWORK SHOULD BE COMPLETED IN WRITING AND ORGANIZED NEATLY IN THE PROPER NOTEBOOK.

But only nerds do homework as soon as they come home. Okay, so I already figured out the answers in my head. Doesn't make me a nerd.

From my window I see Marcus jogging toward my barn. He's dressed in army camouflage. Not real army camo like what's sold at the Army-Navy store. He has on fake camo, like what's sold at the Piperville Mall. Under his left arm he's carrying a Streamer Beamer water gun, his new one with the Boosterama hose attachment.

Game on!

I grab my weapon—my Triple Long Shot Soaker. I got it over the summer with money I saved up mowing lawns. It comes with a neon-green Mega Tank Reserve System and is totally awesome. I open the sliding glass door that Dad installed last year. It leads out of my loft to a ramp that ends up in our backyard. I climb out, run down the ramp, and quickly go around to the front. Marcus is about to knock on the barn door. I take steady aim and let a stream of water rip. I can zero in on a target twenty-five feet away.

"Way. To. Go." Marcus says, not smiling. He shakes the water from his hair, acting like a golden retriever who got an unwanted bath. "I didn't come over to play. I came over to tell you that Cory is fishing on the bridge by Old Man's Creek. I thought we could plan a sneak attack to even the score." Marcus waves his water gun like it's heavy artillery.

"Yo, I'm sorry," I grumble. "Hey Marcus, you think that Cory can make this Antsy Pants thing stick?"

Marcus sighs as if I'm marked for execution. "Until something better comes along. Or until you get some muscle attached to those twigs of yours. Like these." Marcus shows off a bicep the size of a grapefruit.

I ignore Mr. Athletic and refill my water gun at the outside faucet. "You sure this is a good idea?"

"Yes, sir!" He tucks his gun under his arm and salutes. "You're a good shot, Ant. We can take Cory. No pro-blame-o."

Marcus is fearless. I've hoped over and over again that some of his fearlessness will rub off on me. It hasn't happened yet. It probably wasn't happening today.

I follow Marcus until we're about forty feet from the bridge. We drop and crawl the rest of the way like soldiers, with our elbows pulling us along. At the last second, we pop up and let loose a stream of water. Okay, so Marcus pops up. I crouch behind him. I squint, pull the trigger, and pray the battle will be short.

Lucky for me, I hit my target. "Gotcha, Cory! You look like you wet your pants!"

Marcus looks down at me and grins. "Good one, Ant."

Cory runs for cover under the bridge. "Hey, if it ain't Antsy Pants and Marcus Fartcus! Where are you, Ant? You too chicken to show your face? **BWALK! BWALK!** Go back to your barn, chicken."

Marcus sneaks closer to the bridge, then dives behind a bush. I bet he wants to yell something in my defense, but Marcus isn't as quick with his mouth as he is with his feet.

"Shut up, Cory," I yell, still hidden. "This chicken's gonna egg you!"

To my left, I hear snorts coming from Cory's Bully Squad. The Squad is made up of Brad Headley, known secretly to me as Brad Butthead, and Jordon Silverstein, who I call Jordon Jerkenstein. I pump up my soaker and get these two with a solid stream of water. At the same time, Marcus charges the bridge to get Cory, but totally misses.

"Ha. Ha, Fartcus," Cory spits out, not laughing. "You missed me."

"Watch out, or he'll fartcus on you," I shout.

The Bully Squad sneaks up to Marcus and clobbers him with mud balls. And then the fight *really* begins.

I snap on my Mega Tank and jump out of my hiding spot. Marcus and I soak Cory and the other two. The air gets thick with mud and water.

But then Marcus runs out of water. And thirty seconds later, I do, too! Cory, Brad, and Jordon have a whole creek full of mud, so Marcus and I make a run for it. Marcus runs fast and gets away. I don't run fast enough.

I'm no track star. I have hand-eye coordination, but I'm not coordinated when it comes to adding my feet. So, when the mud-flingers chase me, they catch me.

KA-BOOM!

It's not pretty.

They stuff mud everywhere—in my shoes, hair, ears, nose, and armpits. I had a feeling this was the way this day would go down. I should have talked Marcus out of this.

When I finally hobble back home, Marcus is leaning against my barn. He's attached his water gun to our garden hose, and when I collapse on the ground, he sprays me till most of the junk washes off. "We didn't have a chance," Marcus says.

I dig a glob of green and brown slime out of my left ear. "You mean, *I don't* have a chance. Did you hear Cory? I'm doomed to be Antsy Pants *forever*."

"Nah," Marcus says. "Think positive, Ant. It'll blow over soon."

I kick off my soggy sneakers, and spit out, "Ha!"

Marcus shrugs. He heaves his water gun over his shoulder. "We'll fix this. But I've gotta get home. Catch ya later?"

I nod and watch Marcus stroll down our gravel driveway. Marcus is a good friend, but he can't help me. Antsy Pants will be my one thing unless *I can* get rid of it. And I have to ditch it long before I get to middle school next year or I'm dead meat. No way am I entering sixth grade with that name.

I shuffle up the ramp that leads to my room, and I sneak into the shower before Dad sees I've been used for target practice. I put on clean shorts and a plain blue t-shirt but don't bother to comb my hair. It sticks up all over the place whether it's combed or not. I throw on a Phillies baseball hat and press it down. Hard.

I sit in a beanbag chair and reach for my notebook—the *proper notebook,* so I can write down the answers to the math problems I had figured out earlier. I see my doodles and a smile sneaks out. They're pretty hilarious. I flip to a clean sheet and let my pencil skip across the page. I don't

even think about what my hand is doing. The doodle takes on a life of its own. It stars Marcus as a fisherman. He has on a tux, like James Bond wears. I make Cory the bait. Cory is a worm with straggly blond hair and an ugly face. In fact, Cory's so ugly that only humongous man-eating fish want to bite that hook. I draw fierce hammerhead sharks, tiger sharks, and bull sharks. They look extremely hungry and are circling under Cory.

Okay, so what if sharks don't live in creeks? It's a doodle. *My* doodle. By the end of the page, half of Cory is stuck inside a smiley great white, and the other half is begging for mercy.

I feel better. Much better.

CHAPTER FIVE

SUCKER PUNCHED OR SOCCER PUNCHED?

The workload in fifth grade makes my head hurt. I constantly rub my eyes to clear things up. Doesn't always work. And I'm antsier than ever. So is everybody else. Marcus gives anyone the Evil Eye of Death if they call me Antsy Pants. It makes some of the wimpier kids think twice. Cory and the Bully Squad aren't in the wimpy category. They yell the name every chance they get. Then there's what happened yesterday. I'd like to forget yesterday. Cory offered five bucks to any kid who writes, "Ant C. Pantaloni has ants in his pants. Antsy Pants! Antsy Pants!" on the Booger Wall in the boys bathroom. Getting your name on the Booger Wall pegs you as the ultimate loser. Some fourth-grader wannabe bully named Adam did the deed. In permanent marker. He spelled Pantaloni "Pantalonely," but I bet he still got his five.

Today is Friday the 13th. Bad luck is getting ready to spread out a welcome mat for me. Something's bound to happen. **TICK, TOCK. TICK, TOCK.** Two minutes until recess. After recess, the day will be more than half O. V. E. R., over, and that means this not-so-great week is soon over, too.

Principal Paulson is trying out a new schedule this afternoon. The fourth and fifth grades are outside at the same time. We rule Carpenter Elementary because we're the oldest, so this makes us happy. The fourth-graders aren't so happy.

Ryan, Nat, Taylor, Zach, Tyson, Brad, Jordon, and Cory form a soccer team and challenge the younger kids. Marcus joins them because Marcus plays every sport. He doesn't care a rat's butt about who he plays with or against. That leaves me walking in circles around the picnic table, kicking a pebble and feeling like a friendless freak. Pantalonely. Perfect. Adam called it about right.

Alexis, Jillian, and Alicia are at another table, whispering and giggling. I wonder what they're talking about and if I should go hang with them. Alexis was in my class last year, but I never really knew her. She's a total brainiac. Rumor has it she's memorized the dictionary and speaks not only English but German and French, too. If I ever get to Paris to see my mom, maybe she can teach me how to say, "*Are you ever coming back, Mom?*"

I notice that Alexis had her hair cut really short over the summer. And she got glasses—purple glasses with silver streaks on the sides. As I'm thinking this, she waves a pinky finger at me. I turn a gross ketchup-y color and find a bigger pebble to kick.

The game is about to start. Marcus yells, "Ant, we need a goalkeeper!" He motions for me to take a place in front of the net.

I jog over to Marcus trying to look as sporty as possible. I want to talk to him without the whole school listening in. "Yo, Marcus," I whisper. "Don't do this to me. You know I stink."

Marcus shrugs. "We're up against the puny fourth-graders, and I'm on defense. Don't worry. I won't let a ball get anywhere near you. We'll destroy them in, like, five minutes."

I'm not totally lost when it comes to soccer. I've played it in P. E., so there is a small part of me that imagines I can do this.

Marcus keeps his promise for the first half, and no balls bounce, roll, or get anywhere within six feet of me. We score two goals against the fourth-graders. Cake. But in the second half, they fly into a juice-box-induced frenzy. Some new travel team superstar, Ricky Whatever, just subbed in on the fourth grade team, and he dominates. He flashes past Marcus then pummels the ball. Right. Into. My. Gut. Although my stomach feels like it caved in two feet, a good thing happened—I stopped the ball from reaching the goal!

For the next play, Travel Team Ricky darts in and out and around Tyson and Cory, our defensive line, and then leaves Marcus in the dust. Ricky kicks the ball over my head and into the far corner. SCORE! Before any fifth-grader can gain control of the ball again, Ricky knocks in two more in a row. We are toast.

The end result is fourth grade, seven; fifth grade, two. It's probably the only time in the school's history that the puny fourth-graders destroyed the fifth grade glory team.

Cory storms across the field. "We lost cuz of you, Antsy Pants!"

I yell, "We lost because you forgot to score a goal." I kick the goal post, but that's a big mistake because now my foot throbs. I hop on my left and try to rub my right.

One cheerleader wannabe chants, "Antsy Pants, Antsy Pants. Dance, dance, dance!" She claps her hands, kicks, and jumps high in the air.

KA-BOOM!

No, *please*. Not this!

I can see the stupid **Cloud of Doom** hovering, ready to swallow me up.

Five more girls add to the cheer. "Antsy Pants, Antsy Pants! Dance, dance, dance! Let's all dance the Antsy Pants dance."

I want to shrink to the size of a blade of grass. The chanting goes on for thirty long seconds before the recess lady blows her whistle.

"Line up!" she shouts.

Thank you, Mrs. Recess Lady. Couldn't you have blown that whistle forty seconds ago?

In line, Marcus slaps me on the back. "Don't let it get to you. At least you got Cory to shut up." I shrug and keep intense eye contact with my sneakers.

Language Arts

Back in the classroom, it's time for language arts. I listen, but only halfway. Mrs. Merryweather is still stuck on stupid review stuff. On the front cover of my L. A. folder, I start to doodle. The faster my pencil moves, the easier it is to forget what happened on the playground. I make myself into a soccer net that comes to life. I try to swallow up the fourth-graders, but the soccer ball turns into a monster and eats me. I flip the folder to the back side to start another drawing. In this one, I turn myself into a space knight who wants to rescue Alexis from the soccer ball monster, but she rescues me instead.

"Class," Mrs. Merryweather whines, "Take out your science folders, please. I have some handouts for you on biomes." She pronounces biomes like *bry-hromes*. Before Mrs. Merry*whiner* comes down my aisle, I exchange my L. A. folder for my science one. I don't mind science. I don't even watch the clock during science. **TICK, TOCK. TICK, TOCK**. It's 2:32 and six seconds. Okay, so I do. Tough habit to break.

"There are six types of biomes," Mrs. Merryweather says. "We have forest, tundra, desert, marine, grassland, and freshwater." She makes her baton weave in and out of her fingers. Does she ever put that thing down? I picture her in full nun gear twirling into St. Joe's, and draw a quick doodle on the back of the handout before I forget how funny that is. I chuckle out loud and cover it up with a fake cough.

For the next hour, we have to look at charts, statistics, and photos. Mrs. Merryweather becomes an in-sane environ-mentalist when she insists we're wrecking Earth.

"Every generation has its responsibility to the environment," she shouts. "We are in for the fight of our life, people! Our planet is precious, people! And it's dying!"

Mrs. Merryweather uses an antibacterial wipe to dab her sweaty forehead. She grabs a pile of papers and waves them under her arms to dry out her hairy pits. Then she passes out the pit papers. "Class, in front of you is an explanation of a project. Read it thoroughly."

I pick up the paper. I swear it smells like hairy Merryweather.

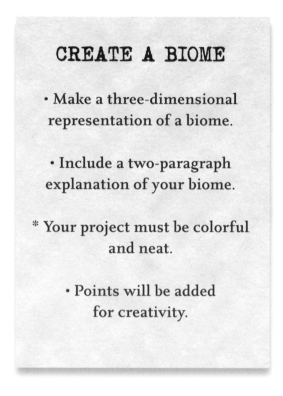

CREATE A BIOME

• Make a three-dimensional representation of a biome.

• Include a two-paragraph explanation of your biome.

* Your project must be colorful and neat.

• Points will be added for creativity.

Big whoop. Another diorama project. Cake.

The class groans like the bored lions at the Philadelphia Zoo. We're all sick of dioramas. Grab a shoebox, throw some toys and junk into it, label things, and it's done. In my mind I play a movie that stars me getting my project finished in ten minutes. But at the end when I'm picturing my A+ grade, Mrs. Merryweather interrupts with a commercial.

"Oh, and people," Mrs. Merryweather says, her voice high like she's on helium, "since you are now fifth-graders, I feel I can expect more from you than a shoebox decorated with non-biodegradable products such as fast food freebies, building blocks, and items from the dollar store. No shoeboxes should be used—plastic, cardboard, or otherwise. Your project must be made completely out of recycled material."

What? Hey, this is different. I quickly sketch a couple of biome ideas. One is of Mrs. Merryweather dressed as a nun, crawling through the desert. In another, Cory has on a soccer uniform and is yelling from a mountaintop.

A third drawing is of Alexis calmly sailing on a lake with her chatty friends.

And the last one is of me, only me. I am biome-less. Which biome should I pick for my project?

The final minutes of school zip by. Once again, I'm glad that walkers are dismissed first. I make my great escape, keep my head down, and talk to no one.

When I get home, Mrs. Urdstrom is there. She has on a shirt with Urdstrom's Housecleaning on it, but I'm not fooled. Mrs. Urdstrom is my babysitter. I've told Dad a gazillion times that I'm old enough to stay home alone. An almost eleven-year-old doesn't need a babysitter. Dad insists Mrs. Urdstrom is there only to clean. She cleans every day that Dad has to work late and Ella Wendy isn't around. She. Is. My. Babysitter!

Ella Wendy got picked to be in the Piper Players, so she's at play practice. My cousin's one thing is being a star. She predicted it. It came true. And she hasn't been quiet about it, either. Everybody in Piperville knows she's the singing and dancing ringleader of some play called *Circus Dollies*. Or was it *Circus Follies*? I wasn't really listening.

Dad has left me a note saying he's at the office and will pick up Ella Wendy, along with pizza, on the way home. We eat a lot of pizza. Don't get me wrong. I love pizza. Along with anything else that comes in a box or carton. But I remember yummier dinners—roast beef with garlic mashed potatoes, three-cheese lasagna, chicken noodle casserole— things Mom used to make for us. She'd say, "Don't eat too much or you'll end up with a tummy ache." And I'd always eat too much.

Thinking about Mom food makes me hungry. I want a steak sandwich from Pat's Steaks—Pat's King of Steaks. When we lived in Philly, we'd go there once a week. Dad would hold me up to the window and I'd shout, "One-wit-out!" Mom and I would split that one. We didn't like fried onions or cheese on ours. Dad would order one-whiz-wit, his usual with fried onions and Cheez Whiz. Half the fun was in the ordering, and we were darn good at it.

When a Mom memory creeps up on me, I get sad. I miss her sometimes.

I go outside to search for biome-building supplies. I decide on a forest biome. Like Mrs. Merryweather, I hate the thought of tree abuse. Dad saves every piece of leftover material from his models of houses and office buildings. He stores it all in an old pickup truck that doesn't run anymore. It's missing an engine, a steering wheel, its hood, and two tires. Dad's supposedly going to fix it up and get it in driving shape by the time I get my license. No way will I be seen in high school in that junker! I'll be driving a black and neon green Jeep with over-sized tires. On the hood and around the sides there'll be an air-brushed fire-breathing dragon or maybe a flesh-eating zombie. A top-rate stereo system will blast out a rap song, and Marcus, in the seat next to me, will use his bullfrog voice to belt out the words. The crowd we hang with will be waiting. We'll hop out of the Jeep without opening our doors, and . . . and . . . I stop. The picture I'm sketching in my head shows Marcus getting all the attention. Yep, that's about right.

In Dad's truck I find five pieces of pressboard. Pressboard is made from recycled cardboard. Hmm, Dad has used it once already for a model, and I'm using it again. I should get extra points for using a recycled recyclable.

I nail the pieces together so they form an open box. As I'm sitting on the grass, a couple of crickets hop over my leg and into the box.

AH HA!

What if I put living creatures in my biome? I'll score creative points if I do this. Crickets only live for a single season anyway, so if I catch some and make a home for them, I can keep them alive all winter long. Live crickets are way better than the ants I had in my ant farm. Those things ate up the gel they were supposed to build tunnels in, and ended up in insect heaven.

I scramble around the yard on my hands and knees grabbing crickets. Not easy! A few finally make it into the plastic zipper bag I got from the kitchen. I put my nose back toward the ground, searching and grabbing again, and crawl straight into a pair of black sneakers. I tilt my face up a little—legs with holey black jeans, black shirt with a vampire on it that says, BITE ME ... straight, messy, blond hair . . . Cory's ugly face.

KA-BOOM!

I hate the thought of facing Cory alone. Where is Marcus when I need him?

"What are you doin' crawling on the ground, dork?" Cory asks. "Lookin' for ants? Lookin' for your relatives, Antsy Pants?"

"You're the one who bugs everybody," I squeak.

Cory steps closer. My insides are mush.

"Ella Wendy here?" Cory wants to know, patting my head like I'm a dog.

"No," I spit out. "Why?"

"I ... came over to ... I wanted to ..." Cory kicks the dirt. "Oh, drat. Just forget it," Cory stammers and slinks away like a poisonous snake.

What the heck was that about?

CHAPTER SIX
A BIOME THAT BITES

It's Saturday and I wake up early to work on my biome project. In fourth grade, we had weeks to turn in a project, but Mrs. Merryweather is only giving us till Monday to work on this one. She's preparing us for the "high expectations of middle school." I have my own high expectations. I highly expect to get rid of Antsy Pants by then.

I doodle my way through breakfast. I need to talk to Dad about finding my one thing. He was a swimmer in school. Maybe I can do that. It's not like swimming is hard or anything. I had lessons in the Philly community pool when I was five. I have a Red Cross certificate somewhere that says I didn't drown. If I could find a pool around here, I could learn the strokes and be on the middle school team, the Dolphins.  Ant Pantaloni—Junior Varsity Swimmer. It's got a nice ring to it. And if my head is soaking wet most of the time, nobody will see my stick-up hair.

Ella Wendy runs into the kitchen and grabs a granola bar. She stops by my seat. "*You* drew that?" she asks, pointing her bar at my picture of the pool.

I nod, then flip my paper over quickly.

"I was trying to pay you a compliment, moron," Ella Wendy says. "I never knew you could draw like that."

I mumble, "Just a doodle," and head for the back door. "I've got stuff to finish up outside before it gets dark."

In the pickup I find the bottom half of an old screen door. It fits across the empty side of my cricket cage, but it needs hinges so I can open and close it. There's an old mailbox in the pickup, so I take the hinges from that and use them. Then I cover the bottom of the cage with dirt and stones. I dig up some wild plants to use as special "trees." Okay, so they're really nothing special. They're twigs and shiny leaves, but they'll do the trick.

I step to the side and give my project the once-over. It isn't awful. It isn't awesome, either. The words "Glassboro Podiatry Care Building: Where we put your best foot forward," are plastered across the top. Uh, oh. I'll need to paint over that.

I find a thick charcoal pencil (in the pickup!) and sketch scenery on every inch of the box, inside and out: a forest, a river with rapids, tents and campers, a ferocious bear, a couple of squirrels, and a mini superhero in a forest ranger outfit. He's got on a green cape made out of leaves and is holding a sign that says, "Save the Forests!" Mrs. Merryweather will definitely add points for that.

Ella Wendy has acrylic paint left over from when she stenciled girly vines and flowers on the wooden walls of her loft, so I get that and paint every inch of my project.

After the paint is dry, I find yesterday's crickets. I can't use them because they've taken an unexpected trip to join my ants in bug heaven. I catch four fresh crickets and watch them check out their home, their biome. They like it! They should be grateful, too, since now they won't become fertilizer before the first frost.

Before I went to bed last night, I researched what crickets eat and drink. I feed my new friends some grass and semi-defrosted broccoli. You'd think that living here in hickville, a place where farmers' markets outnumber convenience stores ten to one, we'd have fresh veggies. But Dad's a city guy. He gets our fresh vegetables from the freezer department at the Super Mart-O-Mat.

I also feed the crickets my leftover breakfast. I had to dig it out of the kitchen trashcan, but these guys can't be picky. A chubby cricket loves some smashed banana the best, so I name him Monkey Butt. Another cricket can't get enough of the gooey oatmeal, so I call him Goo. I bet Monkey Butt and Goo want a drink with their breakfast. We're out of orange juice, so they're getting water. Thing is, you just can't put a bowl of liquid near crickets. The idiots will jump in and drown. I sneak up to Ella Wendy's room and borrow some cotton balls from her make-up drawer. If she gets mad, I'll return them, complete with cricket snot and cricket poop. I soak the cotton balls in water and throw them in. Done! Well, almost. I still have to type the two-paragraph explanation. Cake. Easy A+.

The car door slams. Dad is back from picking up Ella Wendy at play practice. He whistles his way into our barn. Ella Wendy twirls toward me. I check out my cricket cage and pretend I don't see her. There's only so much theater talk a guy can take.

"Crystal likes your dad," she says.

I ignore her. Monkey Butt is crazy-busy, hopping from corner to corner of the box, slamming into the walls and the screen door. He reminds me of me. Maybe he should be called Antsy Butt! Goo sits by the door. He's guarding it. Or planning an escape.

It's like I have pets now. I sort of had a pet in Philly. It was a mouse I named Mickey Cheeses. He showed up only at night. I'd see him when I'd sneak in the kitchen for a midnight snack. We were both obsessed with spicy nachos.

Ella Wendy clears her throat. Dramatically. "I said . . . Crystal likes your dad."

"Who's Crystal?" I ask, adding a big sigh. "What are you yakking about?"

Ella Wendy rolls her eyes like explaining is far too much trouble for her. "Crystal is my drama teacher from New York City. I caught her flirting with your dad."

"Flirting? So?"

"So, I think your dad is absolutely charmed by her."

Ella Wendy's imagination has gone haywire.

"Get lost, Elwen."

Ella Wendy sticks her tongue out at me. "Stop it. I hate that name. It makes me sound like a farmer."

"Wake up," I tell Ella Wendy. "You live in farm country now. You are two shakes of a pig's tail away from wearing overalls and driving the tractor."

Ella Wendy chews on her lip. "You can't be serious." She sits cross-legged on the grass and begins to braid her long hair. "Now, about your dad and Crystal . . . A girl can tell when another girl is flirting."

I keep both eyes on my crickets. I can't have my cousin see that I'm secretly interested in finding out about flirting.

Ella Wendy makes her words come out soft, like she's starring in some stupid romantic movie. "You see, Crystal always picks Uncle Jake out of the crowd waiting to claim their kids. Crystal waves, and I swear she bats her lashes. Uncle Jake looks. He looks away, and then he looks back again. He waves and stares at her likes she's the Mona Lisa. She moves toward—"

"Cut the drama, Elwen."

Ella Wendy growls. "You're no fun at all." She peers into my biome, opens the screen door to adjust a tree, and continues. "Anyway, after, like, ten minutes—men are awfully clueless—Uncle Jake takes the hint and goes over to chat with her. And they talk for an hour. Fifteen minutes, actually. Crystal giggles, Uncle Jake grins, *yadayadayada*. And they don't care that I'm standing next to them, tapping my exhausted toes, hoping that one of them will remember it's time to go home."

"That's it?"

"Between Uncle Jake and Crystal? Uh, huh. That's enough though."

"No, is that all there is to . . . um . . . flirting?"

"That's it, moron," Ella Wendy says. "What's it to you?"

"Nuthin'." I yank off my baseball hat, put it on backwards, and stretch out in the grass.

"Anthony. Dear, sweet, clueless Anthony. Is there a girl flirting with you? Who is it? Alicia Melroy from Everson Street? Tara Niebaum? Tara's sister is my best friend, Tisha. I can get some insider info for you."

"Don't do that! It's none of your business."

"I live in the same place as you. *Everything* is my business." Ella Wendy reaches into the biome again because the tree she fiddled with earlier has fallen over. "This tree is wobbly. You need to make it stand up straighter." Ella Wendy yanks her hand out. "OUCH! Oh. My. Gosh! Something bit me! OMG! Something's in that cage!"

I laugh so hard that snot drips out. "They're crickets. They don't bite."

"Are you sure?" Ella Wendy screams and shakes her whole body as if it's on fire. Her face is ghost white. Like death has snuck up on her. Total drama.

"Yep," I tell her. "Crickets are harmless. You got bitten by a mosquito."

Ella Wendy pouts a sissy girl pout. It makes her look three years younger than me instead of three years older. "That mosquito had my hand for lunch. I can't stop scratching!"

My DOODLES

Please doodle here if this is YOUR
copy of *Just One Thing!*

CHAPTER SEVEN
RED ALERT

By Monday morning, Ella Wendy has a rash shaped like Maryland on her arm, and one shaped like Texas on her left leg. She's got more states in other places she won't tell me about. Dad called the doc yesterday, and now Ella Wendy has to coat herself in a smelly ointment four times a day. She can't go to school.

It turns out the shiny trees in my cricket cage were cleverly disguised ivy. *Poison* ivy. In my old neighborhood in the city, there wasn't enough poison ivy around to make a flea rashy, so it's not like I've had a ton of experience with the stuff. And in the two years I've lived here, nobody's pointed out things in my yard that I shouldn't touch. Heck, I'm sure there's a boatload of other country bumpkin things I shouldn't go near. At least *I* don't have a rash. I have enough trouble.

Before leaving for school, I carefully pick out the ivy and throw it in the trash. Then I swing around to the Vanderbilt's house to grab some new "trees" from their vegetable garden.

I get in the classroom before anybody else. There's a much younger, way prettier version of Mrs. Merryweather sitting on Mrs. Merryweather's desk. She has dark brown hair instead of scrunched gray hair, and ironed skin instead of wrinkled skin. Her feet are tucked under her, and she's sleeping.

Suddenly, the woman's eyes flutter open, sort of in slow-mo. "Excuse me, please. I was finishing up my morning meditation. Hello. Take a seat, Mr. . . . ."

Her voice is *not* like Mrs. Merryweather's. Not like nails on a chalkboard. It's smooth, like a milkshake.

"Mr. . . . ."

"Ant. I mean, Anthony. Anthony Pantaloni."

The kids drift in, coming alone or with best friends. Miss Milkshake hops off the desk, smoothes her skirt, and stands up. She's tall. Six feet tall, probably.

"Class, my name is Ms. Dreyer. I'll be substituting for Mrs. Merryweather today, and throughout the year. I have a chart with your names on it, but I'd prefer it if you introduce yourself. Perhaps you can tell me your nickname and a little about what you enjoy doing."

When Ms. Dreyer says "nickname," my heart skips two beats. Cory is going to find a way to add Antsy Pants to my name. I just know it.

"Young lady in the first row, will you begin, please?"

"I'm Alexis Smucker. I like to be called Lexie now. I've always lived in Piperville. I . . . I play the flute. I like to read. Non-fiction mostly. And when I grow up, I want to be a . . . ."

"Smart Aleck," Emma Brestler blurts out.

I wish Emma hadn't butted in. I wanted to hear the rest.

Emma tagged Alexis, a.k.a. Lexie, as Smart Aleck long before I moved to Piperville. It's more of a fact, than a nickname. Lexie's lucky. Her one thing is something she can be proud of.

Ms. Dreyer moves on. The closer she gets to me, the drier my throat is. It's the Sahara in there. I swallow, but there's no spit. **TICK, TOCK. TICK, TOCK.** It's seven minutes past nine, plus four seconds. I want this to be O. V. E. R., over. I sit on my hands because they're sweating and they itch. Both hands fall asleep. To wake them up I tear out a piece of paper from my notebook and draw Lexie as the president of the United States. I slide it in my desk when Ms. Dreyer moves down the aisle.

Bethany Bellingham is next. She goes into her speech about horses. Whinny sounds start coming from the back row. **WEIGH! WEIGH!** Bethany ignores them, and so does Ms. Dreyer. Ms. Dreyer is the only person on the planet who hasn't heard Bethany's horse stories. Every kid in Carpenter Elementary knows how many different kinds of horses Bethany has, how she brushes her horses' teeth, where she got her horses, what their breeds are, and how many times a week she rides. Horses are Bethany's one thing. We're pretty sick of it.

"Cleopatra is my newest horse," Bethany says. "I call her Cleo. Isn't that adorable? Cleo is Zelda's baby. She was born over the summer in the middle of the night. I got to stay up and watch the vet deliver her. She has bee-u-tee-ful long lashes, a tan coat—that's her color—she doesn't actually wear a coat, and anyway, she is *sooo* cute. Luna, Star, and Neptune are very jealous, so we keep them in a separate barn."

When Bethany starts talking horse, there's no stopping her. If I weren't such a polite kid, I'd call her Horse Teeth. Her teeth could rent their own stable.

"I will be a horse-lover for the rest of my life," Bethany states. Bethany swings around and points to me. "And behind me is . . ."

I croak out, "Anthony Pantaloni. Some people call me Ant. I moved here in third grade. I like to—"

"Eww!" Bethany squeals. "What's on your hands? Is it a flesh-eating disease? Stop scratching it. It might be contagious."

"What? I can't help it," I snap at Horse Teeth. "It itches!"

A siren goes off in my head: *Red alert! Red alert! Poison ivy? Poison ivy!* Seconds later, I fly out of my seat, and tell Ms. Dreyer I have to see the nurse. She waves me toward the door.

From the hallway I hear Cory. "Antsy Pants has the runs! Go, Antsy Pants! Go!" The kids crack up.

KA-BOOM!

It's not like I didn't see this coming.

In the nurse's office Nurse Angelo can't find any lotion to stop my itching. She phones Dad, hands me a dismissal note, and says, "Go home." A half-hour later, Dad shows up and drops me off at our barn.

"Ella Wendy can watch you today," he says. "I have to get to work. Don't give your cousin any trouble. The doctor said that she probably had a bad case of poison ivy before this. Now her body is more sensitive to it. You've never had poison ivy, so yours isn't so bad."

I'm not really listening a hundred percent. Cory's Antsy Pants chant is still ringing in my ears. Part of me is glad I got sent home. The other part is mad. It stinks that I got up early, got ready for school, and got there, only to have this happen. There wasn't a sign of poison ivy anywhere—and I mean *anywhere*—on my body when I was in the shower this morning.

Ella Wendy is slumped on the living room couch, digging into the bottom of an extra-large bag of chips. She's glued to the TV show where everyday celebrities try to be stand-up comedians. It's silly, but

Ella Wendy's not smiling. At least I don't think so. Her lips are swollen from the rash, and the top lip just about touches the bottom of her nose. Her ears look like mangled roses stuck to the side of her head.

"Hey," I say.

Ella Wendy turns and looks at me with her brown puppy eyes. "It's morning. Why are you here? Did you skip school?"

I hold up my hands, so that she can see my rash.

"Oh, so you got it, too. There is a God."

"So far, it hasn't taken on a life of its own, like yours. But an hour ago it was a couple of pink spots. Now, it's showing up on my arm. I'm supposed to put that junk on it." I point to Ella Wendy's tube of ointment.

"Stop staring at me!" she yells. "I've been turned into an ugly duckling."

"You're quackers, Elwen. It's not that bad."

"Stop calling me Elwen! It is bad, and it's all your fault. I'll miss days of play practice." She sniffles and dabs her nose. "I hope you suffer. Suffer!"

"I'm suffering," I tell her. "But not how you think." I look at the floor. "Hey, Elw . . . Ella Wendy, I've got a question. In middle school, is your name, I mean . . . like, is your identity . . . kind of wrapped around one thing? And is that one thing attached to you forever? Or can you change it?"

"It depends. Take this boy, Nate Jamison. He's in the marching band. I don't expect he'll suddenly become a football star. He's a band geek. Everybody knows him as a band geek. He's got so much talent. And he's cute, too, but that's beside the point. And take Kyra Smith. She plays field hockey, basketball, and softball. It'd be strange if she woke up and changed from being jock girl to band geek. And there's Stella Dilworth. She's overweight, and the jerks call her Stella D'ora like the cookie company. See what I'm getting at? Why do you want to know? You won't see the inside of middle school until next year."

"I've got nothing. I'm not good at anything."

Ella Wendy gets up.

"Don't hug me," I warn her.

She limps over and punches me in the arm. Hard. "That's for giving me poison ivy," she says. "And for being such a moron." Ella Wendy grins. Actually, she only grins as much as her swollen face lets her. "By the time you get to Piperville Middle, things will be different."

"Wanna bet?"

Ella Wendy lets out a snort, and goes back to watching TV.

I need to take a walk, but a loud storm has snuck up the coast, and the lightning is scary. When I lived in the city, lightning didn't bother me. Here, the tree branches look like they're part of a backwoods creature. The Jersey Devil, maybe. I imagine the creature spewing out a bolt of lightning. It hits the barn and we get barbecued.

Instead of going out, I take the rungs of my loft ladder two at a time. I have enough pent up energy to light the barn if we lose electricity. Thinking about what Marcus said about my twiggy arms, I try ten push-ups. Push-ups nine and ten are poor excuses for push-ups. They're more like push-downs. I climb on my bed and attempt a pull-up using the beam on my ceiling. When that doesn't work, I hop off and try a jumping jack, but my feet don't jump when my hands jack. I'm left feeling beat up and with nothing to do. Plus, I stink. I smell as bad as Leon Archer, the only boy in fifth grade who hasn't discovered deodorant.

I turn on my computer. Maybe the Internet can solve my not-having-a-one-thing problem. What should I put in the Google search box? *Loser boy needs a claim to fame? Dumb things smart kids can do with their lives? Getting a life before middle school? How to kill a nickname?*

I tap the off button. This is not a search engine thing.

Ella Wendy's medicine is working on my rash, so I'm not spending every minute scratching. Still, I can't help but replay what happened in school. My cousin is right. I am a moron, a chicken-poop-antsy-pants-poor-excuse-for-a-fifth-grader moron who is clueless about most things.

I find an unused sketchbook somebody bought for me years ago and start to draw.

I make a slew of ridiculous-looking crickets and call them the Kookies. The Kookies are evil and they grow poison ivy, wrap it up as lettuce, and sell it to people in the Super Mart-O-Mat. The poison ivy doesn't make them itch. It turns unsuspecting customers (who look like kids in my class) into booger-infested gargoyles, bloodthirsty mosquitoes, and deadly dragons. Bethany's a dragon with a horse's tail, ears, and teeth. I draw Ms. Dreyer as a flying fortuneteller with a peace sign for a crystal ball. She discovers the crickets' evil plot, gathers a force of superhuman kindergartners, and saves the day.

I stare at my page and realize that every cartoon I draw has a hero. And that hero is never me.

CHAPTER EIGHT
THE CAT'S OUT OF THE BAG

Another minute of hanging out with my cousin and I would've been ready for *America's Looniest*, that new reality show where people pretend to be insane to win a million dollars. For the last two days, Ella Wendy has been using me as her audience so she can practice her stage presence. Yesterday I brought in substitutes. Aside from the clapping elephant I've had since I was three, I lined up two robots, four Star Wars guys, and a bunch of sock puppets from the bottom of my sock drawer.

Last night, when Ella Wendy came hunting for me, I faked an emergency case of diarrhea, ran to the bathroom, and sat on the toilet lid drawing more cartoons starring the Kookies. I made fart noises using my hand and armpit. FaRrrRT! FaRrrRT! Thanks go to Marcus for teaching me that. It worked because Ella Wendy kept shouting things like, "Can you be any grosser?" and "Uncle Jake needs to get rid of that stupid sheet and put up a real door!"

Today I'm back at school and so is Mrs. Merryweather. Right before dismissal she tells everybody to sit still and listen carefully. She folds her hands on her desk. It's not a stretch to imagine her as a nun, like she was when she taught Dad.

"Class," she says, "I have an announcement."

Nobody listens to announcements. Today, Finn, a.k.a. Fishboy, is turning his eyelids inside out. Totally awesome! Just try to keep your attention on the teacher when that's happening. Impossible!

FISHBOY!

Mrs. Merryweather clears her throat and stands up with her hands on her hips. This is standard teacher body language for Pay Attention Or You Will Miss Something Important. It's really hard to tear my eyes away from Finn's.

"Soon," Mrs. Merryweather begins, "I'll be taking an extended leave of absence."

Alicia waves her hand wildly. "Are you going to be absent for a long time?"

A snort comes from Brad. I have a hard time not laughing, too. Alicia is about as bright as a worn out glow-in-the dark star sticker.

Lexie frowns at Alicia. Then she raises her hand, and Mrs. Merryweather calls on her. "Why are you leaving?" Lexie asks.

"I'm taking time off," Mrs. Merryweather explains, "because I'll be in the hospital having surgery and will be out for several weeks."

"Are you sick?" Lexie wants to know. You've got to respect a girl who doesn't give up until she gets all the answers.

"No, not really," Mrs. Merryweather says. She fidgets with her baton. "It's personal."

Yuck. That shut everybody up. Everybody except for Emma, who smirks at Lexie. "*Smart . . . Aleck.*"

Mrs. Merryweather makes her eyebrows into a unibrow. "Ms. Dreyer will be the permanent substitute."

"Hurray!" the class cheers. I almost feel sorry for Mrs. Merryweather, what with her being ancient and probably having surgery on her old lady parts.

Mrs. Merryweather shuffles papers and hands the pile to the first kid in the row. "There's an additional piece of information I need to go over with you before dismissal. Since Carpenter Elementary got a new wing added on over the summer, the administration thought it would be fitting to grow with the times and allow a school mascot."

"What's a mascot?" Alicia asks.

Ryan answers. "It's like what colleges have. My sister goes to Penn State and they have a big cat as a mascot."

Jordan Jerkenstein lets loose with a couple of meows.

Lexie waves her hand. "It's not that kind of cat. It's a lion, a Nittany lion, to be exact."

"Thank you, Ryan and Lexie," Mrs. Merryweather says. "A mascot can be an animal, a person, or even an object. Anything that represents a group. The group in this case is the student body of Carpenter Elementary. Mascots are supposed to bring luck and happiness. The teachers came up with an adorable smiling barn for a mascot. It had two large four-leaf clovers for eyes. But young Principal Paulson has more . . . more . . . contemporary plans for this very traditional school of ours. He's looking for a mascot that is entertaining. He wants it to look both intelligent and light-hearted, for he believes that would be a true representation of the FUN we have here in school." Mrs. Merryweather blurts out the word fun like it's a killer noun.

I look at the paper that got tossed to me. Mrs. Merryweather should have used a different font. Some of the letters seem jumbled up against others. I have to squint to read.

Mrs. Merryweather rambles on while a dozen mascots parade around my brain.

"Isn't that exciting?" Mrs. Merryweather asks.

What? What's exciting? I didn't hear what Mrs. Merryweather just said. And I can't blame Fishboy because his eyelids are planted on his eyeballs and he's sound asleep. What did she say?

"Yo, Lexie," I whisper. "What's exciting?"

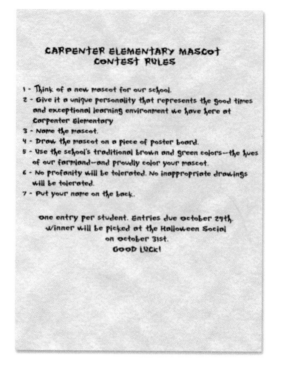

"Dan Wharton is helping the principal pick a winner. Who is that?"

"Dan Wharton? Really? I saw his picture on the front of the *Jersey Herald* this week. One of his paintings just sold for half a million dollars. He's coming here?"

"Guess so," Lexie said. "What's it to you?"

"Nuthin'," I say.

Everything, I think. Dan Wharton is famous! And I might get to meet him!

That afternoon, I race through my homework. I memorize stupid facts about the Egyptians. I wish I had a book that tells me exactly how the Egyptians turned their dead into mummies. Pictures of blood and guts on every page would make everything better. I also answer questions on magnetism for science. Cake. And work out seven math word problems. More cake.

I have to find Dad so I can tell him about the mascot contest. We'll need poster board from the store. And some pencils with decent erasers.

I doubt these things are in the pickup, but I can't rule that out. I want to talk to Dad about becoming a swimmer, too. I really believe that swimming could be my one thing, my ticket to middle school fame. Climbing down from my loft, I hear Dad talking on the phone.

"Who is this? And you want to speak to my niece? Hold on. Anthony, have you seen Ella Wendy? There's someone named Cory who wants to talk to her."

"Cory? Cory Bennett?"

"Yes, that's who."

"Why?"

"Didn't say." Dad scratches his bald spot.

"Hang up," I tell him. "Cory Bennett is T. R. O. U. B. L. E., trouble! Besides, I saw Ella Wendy take off a while ago. She went to Tisha's."

"Trouble? Good info, son. I'll take it from here." Dad puts the phone to his ear. "I'm sorry, but my niece isn't around. May I take a message?" He's quiet for a minute.

Cory's up to something, I bet.

"Uh, hunh," Dad says. "We'll see."

What is Cory talking about for so long?

Dad sighs. "Alrighty then, good-bye." He hangs up.

"Well?" I ask.

Dad taps a pencil on the table. "I don't know what's going on, but it sounds like Cory wants Ella Wendy to be part of some scheme. I wasn't born yesterday, you know."

"Yes, you were, Dad. You don't have a clue. Cory is a jerk." Scheme to Dad would be sneaking out for ice cream. Scheme to Cory could be super-glueing Ella Wendy's braids to her neck for the fun of it.

"Hmm . . ." Dad says, "maybe Cory Bennett isn't as fortunate as you."

"The Bennetts live in Sandpiper Reserve, Dad. They're fortunate!"

"I wonder if you and Ella could help Cory somehow."

"Cory is a bully. Bullies don't need help."

"I see," Dad says. "I suppose Ella Wendy should keep her distance then." Dad looks straight at me. I can almost see the light bulb that has gone on in his brain. "Sounds to me like you have first-hand experience with this kid."

So here's the part where we have our father-son talk. Why do I feel like such a loser in front of my own dad?

"Cory tagged me with this stupid name the first day of school. Now I'm stuck with it."

"And . . ."

"It's Antsy Pants."

"Antsy Pants?" Dad asks. I swear I see him covering up a grin. "Yikes. What'd you do to get that name?"

"I jumped out of my seat and **KA-BOOM!** Cory calls me Antsy Pants. That's who I am now, and guess what? I've got nothing else! You were a swimmer, Ella Wendy is an actress, Marcus is a super-athlete. I need Just. One. Thing. One thing to be known for."

"I don't know what to say," Dad says.

Perfect. So much for fatherly advice. I pound my fist into my thigh. "I need to own *something*. Make it mine."

"You can have the truck," he says, winking.

"That's not what I mean!"

Dad takes my baseball hat and puts it on. He looks silly. He wants me to laugh. I don't. "Oh, Ant, I'm just joking around. I'm sorry. Is it really that bad? What can I do to help?"

I grab my hat and smash it on, backwards. "Remember when I took swimming lessons at the pool in Philly?"

"Your mom took you to those."

"Well, I liked the pool. If I could get myself into swimming shape, learn the strokes, and how to race and stuff, I could try out for the middle school team at the end of this year. I can't go to middle school known as Antsy Pants."

"Swimming is great!" Dad says, a little too enthusiastically. "I'll find a swim class for you. You'll have to go every day. You'll have to work hard." Dad heads for his computer.

I head for a snack. Talking about exercise makes me hungry.

Please doodle here if this is YOUR
copy of *Just One Thing!*

CHAPTER NINE
GO, FISH, GO!

Two weeks later, I'm sitting by the side of the pool taking a breather. It's day three of practice, and I'm wondering if the clock has stopped working. **TICK, TOCK. TICK, TOCK.** It's exactly quarter till five in the afternoon. Fifteen minutes to go. Fifteen long, wet minutes.

I thought swimming would be cake. It was cake when I was a little kid. What the heck happened? My arms do what they're supposed to do, but my legs have a mind of their own. I'm a spastic robot made up of heavy, sinkable metal. The seventy-year-olds doing aqua aerobics in the therapy pool are more coordinated than I am. But I'm not giving up. Swimming could still be my one thing.

"Anthony," screams my instructor. "Get in the water! You may as well work on your butterfly. Nothing else is coming along for you. Try to swim like something other than a dead fish, please."

Nice guy, my instructor.

I slide into the freezing cold water, but hear my name called again.

"Ant, is that you?"

It's Marcus, and he has on a bathing suit. "Yo, what are you doing here?" I ask.

Marcus shrugs. "What do you think I'm doing here?" He flicks the top of my head with his pointer finger and thumb.

I swipe his hand away. "Why are you here? You're not a swimmer. Are you?"

Marcus sits down and dangles his feet in the water. "My mom's been looking into college scholarships. Can you believe it? What parent of a fifth-grader does that? She found out that colleges give out a lot of swimming scholarships, so here I am."

KA-BOOM!

Marcus has stolen my brand new one thing. "You've got hockey and soccer," I say, "and aren't you starting basketball soon?"

Marcus nods. "And swimming."

Don't get me wrong. Marcus is my best friend. But right now, I want to dunk him until his lungs come up through his throat. I can't look him in the eye.

"What's your best stroke?" Marcus asks.

"Floating."

Marcus laughs. "Floating is not a stroke. You wanna race?"

"I can't," I tell him. "I have to be a butterfly."

"No pro-blame-o," Marcus says, "If you want, I can help. The butterfly is my best stroke."

"Of course it is," I mumble.

I show Marcus what I can do. I pull my arms up out of the water and call up enough muscle to wrap them around to the front. I do a dolphin-like kick with my legs glued together like I'm supposed to do, but that kick doesn't make me go farther, it makes me sink. I sniff in instead of out and end up with a nose full of watery chlorine. I blow it out. Booger slime smears across my cheek.

Marcus stands in the shallow end, hands on his hips. "Maybe butterfly's not your stroke. You've gotta be really coordinated. Tell the instructor you want to work on breast stroke." He slaps me on the back and dives in the lane next to me. In minutes, he's butterflying wall-to-wall like a superbug.

"Show off," I yell. He's mostly underwater and doesn't hear me. Probably a good thing.

Maybe I should try the breast stroke. Just thinking of saying "breast" out loud makes my face hot. I invent a stomach cramp and complain to my instructor. He says I can hang it up for the day. What he doesn't know is that I'm hanging it up for good.

I let Dad have the I-don't-want-to-be-a-swimmer news as soon as he picks me up. He understands. Either that or he likes being the only Olympic swimmer wannabe in the family. On the drive home, he switches the subject and tells me about an ad he saw in the *Jersey Herald* for a new gymnastics center that opened recently.

I turn to face him. "Gymnastics? Are you kidding? *Girls* do gymnastics!"

"Calm down, son. So do boys. Think of the rings, the parallel bars, the horse. I've seen you trying to build up your strength with push-ups and pull-ups. Gymnastics is all about strength. When we get home, Google Koller's Gymnastics. Click on "For Kids" and then "Boys." There's a video."

I pull my hat over my face, slink down in the seat. "I don't know about this, Dad."

Dad doesn't push. He turns on the radio, and I stare out the window. Gymnasts are buff. And no water is involved. And there is no way Marcus has time for gymnastics, too.

Once back in my room, I make a quick doodle of myself flying through the air on the rings. My powerful shoulders make a humongous T across the top of my body and my shirt barely fits. USA is printed across my chest.

The crowd is clapping. A wimpy, cowering Cory is in that crowd. The Bully Squad is there, too, but they're so skinny and weak, they

need to be held up by strings. A puppet master controls them from above. I decide to attach strings to me, too, because these days I don't feel in control of anything. Having gymnastics as my one thing is a stretch. That's as likely to happen as Lexie thinking I'm a superhero.

I turn the page and settle into my beanbag chair. Since I'm already drawing, I should work on my entry for the mascot contest. I rack my waterlogged brain, but my head hurts. Probably the gallons of pool water I sucked in.

I flip the pages of my sketchbook. The mascot flubs I've come up with so far are: a skinny carpenter guy wearing a tool belt and holding a hammer and saw. I named him Bob, but scratched that out because Bob is a builder on the little kids' network. Now his name is Butch, but Butch looks like he's going to hunt people down and fry them up for breakfast. Not going to work.

Mr. Creature Teacher is a dude who holds school supplies in each of his six hands. He has a lopsided smile and green hair that's made out of A+'s, and he's wearing brown khaki pants and loafers. But Mr. Creature Teacher kind of resembles Principal Paulson—a creepy, mutant Principal Paulson.

After throwing the loser entries into the trash, I turn on my computer and click on the Koller's Gymnastics website Dad told me about. There's rock music in the background. Boys my age are flying off a trampoline into a ginormous pit full of brick-size foam pieces. It's a dry pool! Pretty awesome! Other boys are swinging like chimps on the rings. A muscled-out instructor is demonstrating how to do a handstand on the vault. Everybody is smiling and laughing—laughing a little too much?

Okay, so it doesn't take a nuclear nerd to see I am not a gymnastics kind of kid. But for some stunts in gymnastics you need either your arms or your feet. Not both at the same time. And no one in school does gymnastics. Do they?

MR. CREATURE
TEACHER

My
DOODLES

Please doodle here if this is YOUR
copy of *Just One Thing!*

CHAPTER TEN
ALL EYES ON ME

Ms. Dreyer is rambling on that Mrs. Merryweather didn't get the chance to grade the biome projects before leaving. Ms. Dreyer says she'll have them done by tomorrow, and apologizes for the delay. It doesn't matter who grades it. I feel an A+ coming. Ms. Dreyer also tells us about a test on punctuation that's on Tuesday. More easy review stuff. Cake.

The biome project gets me thinking about farmland. Farmland gets me thinking about a new idea for a mascot. It's a cow. We're in the country, so a cow could be a good mascot. Everybody here loves cows. Everybody except me. Our school is next to a farm that has a thousand cows. If Farmer Lannigan lets his herd graze out by our playground, we end up reeking of cow poop. Marcus and I used to say, "Later, Stinkygator," like it was our own personal joke. Most of the kids who have lived here forever don't notice the smell anymore. After a couple of years, I still do.

I name my mascot Nellie. Nellie is a friendly cow with purple glasses and short hair. She reminds me of Lexie because she's pretty. I don't add any more details because the lines are starting to blur and my eyebrows ache.

At recess, some of the girls set up an obstacle course that involves the monkey bars, the swings, six hula hoops on the ground, and the slide.

I am not a bragger like Ella Wendy, but I am good at obstacle courses. I can run through an obstacle course like a cheetah in a jungle. I've had practice. Mom and I used to make up these awesome courses during our walks in the city. We'd balance on curbs and pretend to be bad pirates walking the plank; we'd hop on park benches and scare the imaginary crocodiles below, and we'd climb through the big storm drains, pretending they were secret spy caves. If I'd fall and get hurt, Mom would fix me up, telling me how strong and brave I was. She'd find a long crack in the sidewalk and say I was so strong that my fall broke the sidewalk. She made me feel like Superman.

The girls are having a blast with their course. The boys join in because there's no way the girls are allowed to have more fun than the boys. I've got a good feeling about this. Anthony Pantaloni, Ultimate Obstacle Course Star. Now that's one thing I can live with.

We watch the girls compete and Lexie makes it to the final elimination. Now it's boy against boy. The winner of the boys will go up against Lexie!

Ryan totally rules over Butthead Brad, his only real competition. But Brad has a close encounter with the slide and wails like a crybaby. He probably needs three or four stitches. He'll love that. Stitches are a bully's honor badge.

By some miracle I beat Ryan and that leaves me and Marcus in the finals. Figures.

In seconds, Marcus gets wiped with the dust from my sneakers. Is he letting me win? Just as I'm doing the football move where you put your left foot in a hula hoop and your right in the next, I trip.

KA-BOOM!

This is the part where I look like a total wheeze-bag in front of Lexie. And Marcus reigns as Mr. Athletic. But as I get up, I don't see Marcus anywhere in front. I turn around to see him puking his guts out by the swings. I thump the side of my head with the heel of my hand to make sure it's not my imagination. Then, not wanting to waste another second, I sprint to the finish line. Okay, so I'm not that good of a friend. But how many times in life do you get this chance? Nobody is at the finish line to cheer for me. They're watching Marcus. Marcus is a train wreck. People watch train wrecks.

"I'm sick," Marcus complains.

"He's sick," Tyson yells.

"Stop throwing up all over our game," Alicia says. "That's not polite."

A second-grade teacher, who's helping the recess lady today, runs over and takes Marcus by the hand. His face is the color of concrete. He has the look of a two-year-old who's being pulled away by his mommy.

"It's you and me in the finals," Lexie says, cheerfully. She pushes her purple glasses up her nose and grabs my arm. "Let's hurry up. We can finish before the whistle."

"But there's Marcus puke on the course," I remind her.

"So?" Lexie reties her pink and white sneakers. She jogs to the starting line and waves me over.

I'm in this weird place. I want to win. And I don't want to win. Should I even try to beat Lexie? I can tell this game is important to her. She's already Smart Aleck, the IQ-off-the-wall kid. She doesn't need to shake that one thing and get another. Does she want to be Fastest Girl? Toughest Girl? Girl Who Can Beat A Boy Girl? What should I do? Win or lose on purpose?

We take off, and are matched up pretty closely until . .

Lexie loses her footing while weaving in and out of the three swings, and **SPLAT!** She's *vomitized.*

The kids are laughing like hyenas. I don't join in. Nobody goes to help Lexie. Not even her best friend, Jillian. I stop short of the finish line and jog backwards to Lexie. She's covered with tan puke. It's everywhere—on her shoes and pants, on her polka-dotted shirt, on her glasses, down her neck, and in places I can't see. But she's not crying. Normal girls cry over stuff like this, don't they?

"C'mon," I say. "I'll walk you in."

"Ant, you so won, you know," Lexie says.

"Nope, there wasn't a winner," I tell her. "You can't have a winner in an unfinished race."

"Well, actually, I recently read a debate—"

"Give it up, Lexie."

Lexie walks a couple of steps, stops, and says, "Hey, thanks. You're like a knight in shining armor."

I gulp. Me? *Me?* I stare at the doors to the school. I can't talk. Words have taken a vacation somewhere south of my gut. It's a really long walk into the school and down the hallway to Nurse Angelo's office.

Back in class, I feel like a king. I'm wrapped up in an after-recess doodle that shows me with a huge crown sitting on the throne looking out a castle window at my playground kingdom.

Our take-home papers are sitting on my desk. Ms. Dreyer has graded our tests and classwork. I go to shove them in my backpack and see two Cs! A smiley face sticky note is stuck to one, and on it Ms. Dreyer has written, "Please see me."

I have never gotten a C in my whole entire school life! My stomach churns. *CHURRMURR!* With the luck I've been having, somebody's going to hear it and think I'm farting. It's the first day of school all over again. I stay behind after dismissal and shuffle up to Ms. Dreyer's desk.

"You wanted to see me?" I ask politely. Very politely.

"Oh, yes, Ant. I'm worried. I grade on accuracy as well as neatness, and I've been disappointed in your work lately. Are you having trouble understanding any of the material I'm covering?"

"No."

"Let's take a peek at this science paper with the chart. You entered in the answers to our lab on magnetism, but they're in the wrong column. On this math paper here, every six looks more like a zero, and every three an eight. I can't decide if it's sloppy penmanship or mistakes."

"What? I don't make dumb mistakes!" I say, a little too loudly.

"See for yourself."

I pull the papers right up close to my eyes, then push them away. My messed up numbers glare at me. She's right. I'm an idiot.

"I've looked at your grades from last year and the year before. You have a good record. You usually excel in every subject. There may be something more going on here."

"There is?" I ask. "Like what?" The words "brain tumor" pop into my brain.

Ms. Dreyer rifles through a couple of folders. "Back in third grade, did you have a vision test with the rest of the students?"

"No, I moved here in the middle of third grade. Besides, I can see fine. Watch me read the lunch menu on the blackboard: Macaroni and sneeze. *Sneeze?*"

Ms. Dreyer turns toward the blackboard. "Looks like somebody's been playing around with the menu. I'm afraid it does say sneeze. Ignore that. Go on."

"Peas, Buttered Bread, Milk or Chocolate Milk, Choice of Lice Pudding or Cookies. *Lice* pudding?"

Ms. Dreyer chuckles. "That's what it says. I've got to find this joker. Keep going."

"Cost is $1.50. Ice cream is extra. This lunch menu is subject to change."

Ms. Dreyer doesn't look at me. She's busy writing on a slip of paper.

"I got the words right, right?" I ask.

"Ant, that menu is six feet away and is written in bright white, block letters. I'm worried about your close up vision. You may be farsighted."

"But I draw all the time. I can see close up."

I don't get it. What's farsighted mean? I don't want to sound any more stupid than I already feel, so I stay quiet.

"If possible," Ms. Dreyer continues, "I'd like you to visit an eye doctor this weekend. The eye center at the mall usually has openings on Saturdays. I have a sneaky suspicion we'll get to the bottom of your grades soon. Take this note home and get it signed."

My
DOODLES

Please doodle here if this is YOUR
copy of *Just One Thing!*

CHAPTER ELEVEN
IT'S AWKWARD

Yesterday ended up in the toilet. Today will be another toilet day. Dad called the eye doc the minute I gave him Ms. Dreyer's note, and now we're heading to my appointment. What a waste of a Saturday. It's eighty degrees. That's water gun weather, and lucky me, I get to spend it in a stupid doctor's office.

A nurse wearing a daisy uniform puts drops in my eyes. They make my eyes feel gooey, like they've been coated with melted butter. It feels like my eyelids are slipping off. She has me sit on a stool and look into two eye-checking machines. She makes a big deal of how they won't hurt me, and that I shouldn't be scared. What the heck? Can't *she* see? I'm not a baby.

When I have to stick my head in a third machine, the daisy nurse tells me to expect a puff of air in my eye. This makes me nervous! One slip of that pressure button and this thing could pop out my eyeball.

Doctor Anderson comes in next. She smells really good. Like peaches. She checks my eyes using a bright light. Then I read letters as a bunch of different lenses click in front of me. "You must be getting headaches," Doctor Anderson says, not smiling. How does she know this? Can she see my brain tumor?

When the doc is done, she calls for Dad and they go into another room. I pop up from the seat and pace like a mouse that can't find the end of a maze. What are they talking about? Am I going blind? Something bad showed up in the eyeball-zapping machine, didn't it?

TICK, TOCK. TICK, TOCK. Five minutes tick by. Then six, and seven. I sit down again, put my feet up, and try to concentrate on happy stuff like rollercoasters, popcorn, and 3-D robot movies.

At 10:37 and forty-two seconds, Dad and the doc come back. "Anthony, there is good news and bad news," Dr. Anderson says.

I blink at the blurry doctor and wonder which news is coming first.

"Everything looks healthy," she explains. "Your far-away vision is adequate, as well. But your close up vision needs tweaking."

"Tweaking?"

Dad chuckles. "You need glasses for reading and doing schoolwork."

KA-BOOM!

What else am I in for this year? Fifth grade stinks!

"Seriously?" I yell. "That's horrible! I'll be a major geek."

"It'll be fine," Dad says. "I wear glasses for close-up work. Like me, you won't have to wear them every minute of the day."

This does not make me feel better.

I walk with Dad to the front office where they have rows and rows of glasses. I try on pair after pair. They're all dumb. Each pair turns me into a human fly. Ant Pantaloni, Italian fly. Caution: geek ahead!

Finally, I find a basic brown pair and try them on.

"They make you look smart," Dad says.

"I'm already smart," I snap. "I can't get these. They hurt my ears."

A man with poufy hair and gold glasses pulls me to the side. "The designer frames are quite popular," he says. "Try these."

Dad shrugs. Dad wouldn't know popular if he stepped in it.

The man hands me black frames that actually fit my face and don't hurt my ears. I lean in close to the mirror. "These are okay," I say.

Dad's happy I've found a pair. He isn't happy that they cost $200.

On the way home, we stop at Koller's Gymnastics. Dad has signed me up for a trial lesson, and I'm kind of excited to go. It almost makes me forget there are glasses with my name on them sitting in a bag next to me.

In the locker room I change into shorts and a matching Koller's t-shirt and check out my reflection in the mirror. The eye drops have worn off so things aren't blurry anymore. I can see really clearly that I don't look very athletic. I jog out to the gym floor and pretend to be as coordinated as my clothes.

"I'm Coach Martin," a man says, shaking my hand hard enough to wobble my entire body. "Stand on the mat. We're about to warm up."

The fluorescent lights that hang from the ceiling are so bright. The daisy nurse told me my eyes would be sensitive for a while. I squint to block out the glare.

We do push-ups; we run; we do jumping jacks. My legs still can't jump when my arms jack, but nobody notices. We sit on the mat and stretch. Coach Martin has us do twenty sit-ups. I like sit-ups. I can do fifty. Cake. So far, so good.

The first piece of equipment we learn about is the pommel horse. I don't have a clue why it's called a horse. It's a fat padded bench that's on legs and stands about five feet high. There's a handle on each side shaped like a flattened upside-down U. We have to jump on a mini trampoline and end up between the two handles. Jumping is something I can do. As long as I don't have to add any hands.

Four kids go, one right after the other. Now it's my turn. I run and hit the tramp and hop up exactly where I'm supposed to be—squatting in the middle of the handles. I jump off, go around, and get in line again. Dad's grinning at me from the bleachers. He gives me a thumbs-up sign with two thumbs. I pretend I'm not related to him.

Next, Coach Martin wants us to swing our legs through instead of stopping. The first three kids make it and land on their feet. Kid number four jumps, flips through like a kangaroo, and lands on his butt. He gets up and rubs both butt cheeks.

I try not to think about getting hurt, but I do and that makes me think about my feet. Left foot, right foot, left, right, left, left . . . hop on the tramp, and **SL AM!** My privates smash into a handle! "YeeOUCH!" I scream. Everybody in the gym stops. Everybody stares. A few guys clutch their privates. They know my pain.

Coach helps me down. From somewhere, I hear girls giggling. I finally open my eyes wide and see the same cheerleader wannabes who were cheering at recess. They may have done the Antsy Pants cheer, but I'm in too much pain to hear straight. Why can't I find Just. One. Thing?! Just one thing to do at a place where no one knows me.

I stumble to the mat and glue myself to it. I can't do anything but watch everybody move to the next station. The boys tumble into a foam pit, get out, and head for the uneven bars. When the coach asks me if I'm ready to give the bars a try, I say, "No, thanks!" Even the word bar makes me double over.

Later, in the car, Dad asks, "You going back next week?"

"You going to the moon?" I ask.

"Watch your mouth," Dad says. "Nothing worthwhile comes easy. If you're going to own something, it'll take time, practice, and dedication."

"Gymnastics won't be my one thing, Dad. I feel . . . um . . . awkward doing that stuff." I'm thinking that Dad will buy this excuse.

There's an awkward silence. Dad's probably wishing he was Marcus's father instead of mine. He'd enjoy watching him rule every sport.

I find a felt-tipped pen and an old map in the glove compartment and draw. I turn the winding rivers into monsters and gargoyles. In a couple of minutes, my eyes feel tired and I remember I'm supposed to wear my glasses for close-up work. I find the store bag, open the glasses case, and turn myself into a four-eyed creature. I flip down the visor mirror, then shove it up again. Who is that geek?

MY DOODLES

Please doodle here if this is YOUR
copy of *Just One Thing!*

CHAPTER TWELVE
Too MUCH INFORMATION

For the entire day on Monday, I'm able to be Ant C. Pantaloni, a.k.a Antsy Pants, a kid who doesn't wear glasses. In the morning, we have Big Red visit our classroom. Big Red is a 250-pound drug addict turned speaker. Talk about a one thing! He's here to warn us about drug and alcohol abuse. He gives us a gruesome talk about his horrible life and how he used to live in a box under the Jersey Turnpike. If you ask me, living under a turnpike sounds pretty interesting. Except for when you have to pee in a can and poop in an abandoned parking lot off Interstate 95. If you don't, the other homeless people get mad and set fire to your box.

The whole time Big Red talks, he tries to act like a teenager. "Ya see there, dudes and dudettes," he says, "like, holey moley, my existence was totally and absolutely and disgustingly messed up, ya know? It was nowheresville. Like, I had no life, man."

"He still doesn't," I whisper to Marcus. Vincento, the old man who bags groceries at the Super Mart-O-Mat, has a better life than Big Red.

When Big Red gets to the part about how he quit drugs and now has a steady job as a New York trash man, he grins at Ms. Dreyer. Ms.

Dreyer's cheeks change to the same shade as her apple pencil holder, and I laugh. Okay, so I laugh only on the inside. Big Red actually scares the poop out of me. I can't even squeeze out a giggle. I bet he scares Ms. Dreyer, too. Guess that's the point.

Another assembly comes along in the afternoon. The entire fifth grade splits up into boys and girls. The girls go to the auditorium. The boys leave for the gym. We know what's coming. The boys see a movie called *Our Changing Bodies*. The girls get a different movie, of course. Kids look forward to these assemblies as much as a squirrel looks forward to missing a tree limb. It's embarrassing. No one talks about it. At least a movie is a far-away kind of seeing thing. I don't need my glasses.

At home, Ella Wendy is singing loud enough to make the floorboards creak. I hide in the shed, put air in my bike tires, and adjust the seat. If I make it any higher, it's going to fall off. Maybe I'll ask for a new bike for Christmas—one with a cool suspension system so my butt doesn't hurt when I ride off-road.

When I get inside the barn again, Ella Wendy is still singing. Louder! I can see why she got the lead in *Circus Follies*. She sure can belt out a tune. Plus, she's good. Annoying, but good. When she sees me, she stops singing and follows me like a cat begging for attention.

"Your dad was on two dates with Crystal this weekend," she says.

I sigh, and dive into my after-school bowl of Crunchy Munchkins cereal.

"He had on that kissy face Saturday during rehearsal. And he sang along with the cast. If that wasn't embarrassing! He wasn't here Saturday night when you were at the movies with Marcus, so I know he went on a date with Crystal then. And did you hear him yesterday when he said he was going to St. Joe's to talk to the priest about renovating the admissions building? Well, Tisha said that Melanie said that Julie said that her mother saw Crystal and Uncle Jake at the park. They were having a romantic picnic. Your dad is in love." Ella Wendy stops to take a breath. "What do you think about that?"

Ella Wendy is like a TV I want to turn off. To block her out, I concentrate on the back of my cereal box. There's a picture of a blue and gold robot with wings. A boy younger than me is holding it and the photographer has zoomed in close. Underneath, in big, bold letters, it says:

MEGANOID!

A WALKING, TALKING, FLYING ROBOT JUST FOR KIDS!

"I've got to get this! It even comes with batteries. All for only seven box tops, plus $15, plus tax, plus shipping and handling. What a bargain!"

Ella Wendy grabs the cereal box. "Well, does it bother you?"

"Nope, I don't care that it's for little kids. Robots are awesome."

Out of nowhere, Ella Wendy punches my arm.

"Hey!" I yell. "What was that for?"

Ella Wendy sighs. "You. Are. Hopeless. Haven't you been paying attention to what's been going on around here? You should wear your glasses! You are missing everything!"

"If I did, I'd see what you really look like and have a heart attack." I pile a bunch of cereal on my spoon and shove it in my mouth. "WhAF do YAH want?" I mumble.

"Your dad has a crush on someone. Doesn't that interest you? It's my drama teacher, Crystal. They've been dating. Maybe they're in lo-ov-ve." Ella says love like it's a three-syllable word.

Now I *am* paying attention. I swallow the soggy flakes. "You sure you haven't been sniffing nail polish remover?"

"Mor—" Ella Wendy cuts off mid-moron, takes a deep breath, and tilts her head.

"Anthony. Dear, sweet, clueless Anthony, watch out. A stepmother could be in your future." She gets up to leave. "I have no more time for this. I have to get back to my singing. My show is just weeks away! Write that down. Then put on your stupid glasses and read it. You are coming! And by the way, that kiddie robot costs *seventy* box tops and *$50*."

With that, Ella Wendy flips her hair and dances out of the kitchen. I'm left with an empty cereal bowl and a brain full of romance. Yuck.

I draw a little before bed, trying to put what Ella Wendy said out of my head. I think about tomorrow. Tomorrow is G-Day—Glasses Day. I'll have to wear my glasses to take a test. Either that or possibly flunk for this marking period. If only my glasses gave me superhuman powers. If only they made me invisible.

The next morning, I can't help but watch the clock. **TICK, TOCK. TICK. TOCK**. At eleven-thirty on the dot, Ms. Dreyer puts a two-page test on my desk. She taps the paper, taps her left eyebrow, and winks. I get the message. I'm pretty sure I won't forgive Ms. Dreyer for calling me on this I-can't-see-up-close thing.

"Please remember that this is a timed test," Ms. Dreyer says. "You have twenty minutes. Pencils ready?" she asks. "Begin."

Lexie's pencil scratches across her paper at the speed of light. I look down at my test. There are thirty sentences with wrong punctuation and misspelled words, and I have to fix them. I squint. I blink. I rub my eyes. Nothing helps me see clearly. A comma blurs into a semicolon. An "l" looks like an exclamation point, but I can't be sure. I need my glasses, but how can I put them on without anyone noticing?

I decide to fake a sneeze, so I have a reason to reach into my desk. *ACHOO!* To make sure, I add two more. *ACHOO! ACHOO!* I duck down and pretend to get a tissue. Instead, I slide on my glasses.

"Bless you," Jillian says. "You look different."

"No talking, Jillian," Ms. Dreyer says.

Lexie hands me extra tissues. She points to my glasses and holds her palms up, like she's confused.

I cross my eyes and nod.

Lexie giggles and dives into her test again.

Marcus whispers his bullfrog whisper, "Cool glasses, Ant. You just get 'em?"

KA-BOOM!

Thanks a lot, best friend.

Ms. Dreyer stops the test timer.

Cory swings around and points to me. "Glasses! Antsy Pants got glasses."

All pencils freeze. I freeze, but it's not a chill that's working its way up my spine to my cheeks. It's fire.

"Antsy Pants has four eyes. Bug Face! Bug Face!" Cory shouts.

Ms. Dreyer frowns and motions for everybody to turn over their test papers. "Cory, that'll be quite enough," she says.

Everybody is staring! Enough is enough! I rip off my glasses, jump out of my seat, and march over to Cory, sure that I can pummel that ugly face into smithereens. I tighten my fist. "Leave me alone," I say, gritting my teeth. I open my fist. I tighten it. I open my fist, shake my fingers, and go numb.

I can't do it. I am not a puncher. I can't punch anybody . . . especially a girl.

CHAPTER THIRTEEN
FOUR-EYED FREAKAZOID

Cory shrivels into her chair. Okay, so maybe she doesn't *shrivel*, but she rocks back. The chair goes up on two legs. I secretly hope she falls flat on her stupid brain. She balances there and doesn't move a muscle. Is she scared of me?

I back off when I hear Ms. Dreyer call my name and tell me to sit down. The whole fight takes less than fifteen seconds, but something has changed. Cory's usual smirk is not so huge. And she's quiet.

Ms. Dreyer resets the test timer and we finish our tests. Later, she stops me in the hallway. "Don't let Cory get to you," she says. "The next time you feel angry take a deep breath, then let it out slowly. Think about what might happen if you actually did lose control."

"I'll be okay," I say.

"And Ant, those glasses are terrific!" Ms. Dreyer says, much too enthusiastically.

I don't break into a thank-you smile. I focus on the floor, cram my hands into my pockets, and shuffle off to the cafeteria.

In the cafeteria I go through the lunch line, grabbing anything that's not leftover from the day before. At the end, Cory is waiting for me, sucking cherry fruit drink straight from the carton, no straw. Brad Butthead and Jordon Jerkenstein are being copycats, trying to score good bully points, probably. Cory looks like her old fierce self again. She's her fiercest when she's got the Bully Squad with her. And red liquid dripping from her mouth.

"Hey, Bug Face, think your geek glasses can turn you into Mr. Toughie, huh? Huh, Antsy Pants?"

"Bug off," I say. I go around the Bully Squad and park myself at a table.

Lexie squishes next to me. "You were awesome," she says. "That girl needs to be put in her place. She calls everybody names. This morning, she called Jillian, Silly Jilly, right Jillian?"

Jillian giggles. "I can't help it if I laugh a lot," she says. "I'm a happy kid."

For the rest of the day, I sort of listen to Ms. Dreyer. I'm bored, but there is no way I'll be jumping out of my seat twice in a single day. I doodle off and on. No more headaches now that I wear my glasses. So what if I'm a four-eyed freakazoid? I draw Cory. She's a mangy oinker that's about to become a fried pork chop because a flying robot has his laser trained on her. The robot is me.

Ms. Dreyer hands out the grades for the biome projects. I did get extra points for adding crickets and for doing such a great job decorating recycled material. It's an A+ like I predicted.

If I can predict stuff like this, why can't I predict I won't be a complete loser come middle school?

Nobody is home when I get there. Nobody except Mrs. Urdstrom. I can hear the vacuum vrooming across the wooden barn floor. It's loud and I don't feel like listening to loud. It's a warm fall day. Harvest time. Everything is decked out in oranges, reds, and yellows, and it smells nutty. I must officially be a hick now because I'm noticing how great dead crops smell. If I don't watch it, I'll be wearing overalls and strutting around with a piece of straw hanging from my lips.

Fall isn't a big thing in Philly. It's not like the buildings and sidewalks can get orange, red, and yellow. But fall is everywhere here. It's pretty hard to miss an orange Jersey forest. I put my cricket cage in the shed, then take my notebook and find a big, old oak to draw under. I have to come up with a mascot! I want to enter that contest. On the top of the page I write, "Mascot." It's sloppy, and I put on my glasses before trying to do more. I sketch a roadrunner, a turkey, and a horse. But they're terrible. I move on to pointless doodles. Definitely not mascot material.

I catch something moving. I take off my glasses so I can see far away.

Somebody is walking up my drive. I can't believe it. It's Cory! She's about to knock on my front door! Why can't that girl leave me alone?

I slide behind the tree so its trunk hides most of me. Cory has ditched her usual Gothic clothes. She has on a pink and gray hoodie and jeans, and I think . . . I think she has actually combed her hair into a ponytail. What's up with that?

Mrs. Urdstrom is probably still vacuuming her brains out and can't hear Cory's knock. Cory tries the doorbell. No luck. Then she turns to leave. She has a freaky expression on her face. Like she's mad and sad at the same time. She clomps down my porch steps.

And that's when I sneeze. A real sneeze. *ACHOO!*

Cory snaps up like a rabbit in danger. "Come out!" she shouts.

I walk out from behind my tree. "Why don't you take a long walk off a short plank—a pirate ship plank?" I say. "What are you doing here?"

"Not lookin' for you," Cory says. "Lookin' for Ella Wendy. When does she get home? She still at play practice?"

"How do you know about that?" I ask. "What are you, a stalker? Are you stalking my cousin?" I don't wait for an answer. "My dad knows you're trouble, Cory. I told him the day you called. He won't let you talk to her."

Cory is quiet. Too quiet.

"What do you want with Ella Wendy, anyway? It's not like you two are friends."

Cory inches closer to me. Is she gearing up to clobber me? On the outside, I'm standing my ground. On the inside, my intestines are disintegrating.

"I can sing," Cory says, flatly.

I must've missed something—some part of this conversation. What's singing got to do with anything?

"I wanna be a Piper Player."

My eyeballs pop out in disbelief. "What?" I ask.

And that's when it starts. The singing. Cory is singing *America the Beautiful.* Her voice is strange. It's a stranger's voice. It's not even close to her talking voice. It's . . . it's . . . Well, she . . . she sounds like a pro. Maybe Cory's lip-syncing. Maybe she's got an iPod hiding under that over-sized hoodie. Maybe I've lost my mind.

When Cory finishes, she sticks out her tongue, turns on a heel, and walks away. She leaves me standing there with my mouth open. A hawk could land on my tonsils. I wouldn't feel it.

"Cory," I call, and I can't believe I'm saying this, "Ella Wendy gets home at six."

"Don't suppose you wanna tell her about me," she says.

"Like I said, my dad won't let you near her because of what I said."

"Heard you the first time, Antsy Pants," Cory says.

An idea is growing in my head. An opportunity. "If I get Ella Wendy to come out and tell you about the Piper Players, like how to try out and stuff, you've got to quit calling me Antsy Pants."

"Bite me," Cory says. She sticks out her tongue again then zaps it in, like a frog that just caught a fly. She stares at a cloud that's rolling by. "Well . . . okey dokey, Bug Face."

"And quit calling me Bug Face, too."

Cory scrunches up her nose. Her pea brain is having a tough time. Then she halfway grins, and she spits out, "Deal."

My
DOODLES

Please doodle here if this is YOUR
copy of *Just One Thing!*

CHAPTER FOURTEEN
MORE SURPRISES

Friday over breakfast I tell Dad he was right about Cory. She does need help. I convince him I'm the guy for the job. It's easy. It's not so easy convincing Ella Wendy.

"Why do I need to meet her?" Ella Wendy whines. "Uncle Jake said you told him she was a bully. I don't associate with bullies." Ella Wendy tilts her nose up two inches.

"She can sing," I say. "Really sing. She's *USA Idol* material. Seriously, you should hear her. You'd faint. She wants to be a Piper Player." I sigh, pressing my hands together like I'm praying. "Please talk to her, Elwen? Please, Ella Wendy?" I explain a little bit about the deal that Cory and I have together. I leave out the Antsy Pants disaster and only tell Ella Wendy that Cory's a pain in my butt and won't let up until I set up this meeting.

"Well, I could probably help the poor girl," Ella Wendy says. "I am star material. I have skills. From what you've told me about Cory, I'm pretty sure that she'd benefit from some hair and make-up tips, too. And she'll need to learn to dress properly, speak properly, and learn about stage presence, *yadayadayada*."

"So you'll meet her?" I ask. I don't care a rat's butt about the rest of the stuff coming out of Ella Wendy's mouth.

"Sure," Ella Wendy answers. "Tell her to meet me at five o'clock outside my school today. I'll make her my personal project. In *My Fair Lady*, Eliza Doolittle, an extremely homely girl, turns into a beautiful woman because Henry Higgins transforms her. I'll be Cory's Henry Higgins."

"What?"

"Broadway, moron. *My Fair Lady* is a musical on Broadway."

Ella Wendy starts singing, and I bolt. Mission accomplished.

In no time at all, Saturday rolls around. Ella Wendy corners me before leaving for practice and tells me she was "flabbergasted" when she heard Cory sing yesterday. "We were on Tisha's porch and Cory was singing and this couple walked by and stopped and clapped. You were right. She's pretty good. What exactly is your problem with her?"

"I can't talk about it," I say and make a quick exit. If Ella Wendy finds out about my Antsy Pants nickname, there'll be no end to it.

It's pretty warm for October, so when Marcus comes over, we head for the pond on our bikes.

At the top of the hill Marcus shouts, "Race you in!"

"You're on," I tell him, and I push the pedals hard and fast. We both go like a couple of crazy dirt bike dudes, and yell, "WAH-ROOOM!" A bug plasters itself to my front tooth, but I don't stop. Our bikes plow into the water at exactly the same second and stop dead. Before we keel over, we try to balance there. It's like we're in a hilarious slow-mo movie.

Driving bikes into a pond is awesome. Getting them out isn't. It takes both of us to get one out at a time. Marcus and I finally yank them to the edge and drop on the grass.

"Hey, Marcus, guess what?" I ask, wiping the mud away from my mouth.

"You're gonna be a bike racer like Neil Armstrong?"

"Marcus, you idiot. The biker is Lance Armstrong. And no, I'm not turning into a pro biker. Have you seen what they wear? It's like they've got a diaper on their butts. Anyway, I was about to say

I found out something—something about Cory. You won't believe it when I tell you."

"I'll believe anything," Marcus says.

"She's a singer. I mean, she can actually sing."

Marcus sits up and stares at me like I'm speaking alien. "You're kidding, right?"

"Nope."

"There's more," I tell Marcus. "I made a deal with Cory. If I can get Ella Wendy to help her get into the Piper Players group, that community theater group thing, Cory has promised she'll stop calling me names."

"Ant, that's brilliant. But be careful. I don't trust that girl. Nobody does."

"I hear you. We'll find out if my plan has worked on Monday."

Marcus gets up. "Gotta run. B-ball practice. You wanna come watch?"

"Nope. My dad's in Philly today, and I'm hoping he's stopping at Pat's for my steak wit-out. I don't want to be late for dinner."

"You and your Philly sandwiches," Marcus says and waves good-bye.

I jump on my bike, cruise around the yard, and pretend I'm on a souped-up dirt bike that can splash through mud, cruise over stones, and climb hills with no problem. A while ago, at the bottom of our driveway, I set up a small ramp using a pile of rocks and an old surfboard. I pedal fast for that ramp. When my wheels hit the top, I pull up on the handlebars, hoping to fly through the air and land on two tires. That doesn't happen. My front tire slips off the left edge; I get dumped on the ground and slash my elbow. The cut stings, but stops once I spit on it. It doesn't need stitches. I've got no broken bones. Not even a bruise to prove what a daredevil I am. I'm a daredevil dud.

When I go inside, the phone is ringing. I pick it up.

"Hey, Anthony," Dad says. "Ella Wendy will be there soon. She's getting dropped off by Tisha's mom. She'll make you something for dinner."

"I'm really hungry for a Pat's steak sandwich," I tell Dad. "Aren't you in Philly? Can't you stop there? There are no good steaks in Jersey!"

"Another time," Dad says. "I've got plans tonight. Oh, and I'm bringing home a surprise. I'll be late. You can wait up."

"Really?" I say. Part of me wonders if Mom is coming for a visit. The other part knows that won't happen.

Dad sighs. "It's not what you think. I haven't talked to your mom in six months. You hear from her more than I do."

How can he read my mind, even through the phone? I tell Dad to have fun tonight, and that I can't wait to see his surprise. Then I hang up.

I run up the ladder to my loft, do three pull-ups and ten push-ups, and head for the shower. While I'm waiting for dinner, I want to work out an idea that came to me for the mascot contest. It starts out as a smiley corn stalk. I name him Corny and stick him on a tractor. Not bad. My pencil keeps going, fast, like I'm not even attached to it. In seconds, Corny's leaves have grown and mutated into wild serpents. I make them crawl up the sides of the paper and crash through waves in the Atlantic Ocean. The serpents find the Eiffel Tower and strangle it. Okay, so cornstalk serpents are probably not what Principal Paulson had in mind for Carpenter Elementary's entertaining mascot.

I hear Ella Wendy singing. It's coming from the kitchen. "What are you making?" I yell from my loft.

"Pasta," Ella Wendy says.

"And what?" I climb down to get a better whiff of dinner. "It better be good. I'm starving."

"I'm making pasta and more pasta. And toast. I'm not a chef. I am an actress," Ella Wendy says, losing her patience. She drains the spaghetti and dumps it on my plate.

While I'm waiting for my toast to pop up, I check out my arm in the toaster's mirror-like finish. I make a muscle to see if my bicep is as strong as it feels. Maybe it's the silver, sort of bumpy finish. Maybe

it isn't. All I know is that the muscle that's showing up in there is not imaginary. I do a couple more poses before I hear Ella Wendy yell, "Stop that! It's time to eat."

I open the fridge and grab sprinkle cheese, spicy salsa, some leftover refried beans, and sour cream. I dump it on my spaghetti, swirl it around, and jam it in my mouth. Then I smile a really big smile at Ella Wendy. A really long piece slides out and I suck it in like I'm a mini-vac. "Yum."

"You are gross," Ella Wendy says.

"You can't cook," I say.

"No one ever showed me how to cook," Ella Wendy says. "I am missing a couple of parents, in case you haven't noticed. And it's not like Uncle Jake is some great chef. He has five take-out places on speed dial."

Ella Wendy's frown reminds me I should be nice to my cousin. It can't be easy knowing that your parents live in a combat zone. I swallow my food and, nice guy that I am, I even wipe the sauce from my chin. "Have you heard from them?"

"I got two letters this week, and an email three nights ago. Mom and Dad are exhausted, but not hurt or anything. I told them about my play. I wish they could be here for it."

I search for something to say that will make Ella Wendy feel better. "Dad could take video of you. Or I could. You can send it to them."

"Wow, that would be fantastic! You and Uncle Jake are . . . you're the best."

I smile and lean away from Ella Wendy because I feel a punch coming on. Instead she pushes the spaghetti around and around on her plate, like she's deep in thought. She doesn't take a bite.

"Can I have that?" I ask, poking my fork in her spaghetti.

"Sure," Ella Wendy says, pushing her plate in my direction. "Oh, by the way, I helped your friend, Cory, again today, after play practice."

"She's not my friend, and you know it."

"But she does have talent. She could be a Piper Player. Someday. It's too late for her to be in the *Circus Follies*, though. I feel kind of sorry for her. It's like she wants to change but doesn't know how to go about it. Tisha and I are trying to get her in touch with her feminine side."

I cram more pasta in my mouth. "Yeah, right. FARM-in-ine side," I mumble.

"Ant, remember when you told me you had nothing—nothing that makes you stand out? Well, Cory didn't have anything either. Until now."

"Everybody knows she's been the class bully since forever, Elwen."

"Stop calling me Elwen!" Ella Wendy shouts. "And no one should be a bully. Cory needs to work on being graceful and charming."

"No kidding," I say.

"What if Cory sort of ended up like she is by accident. Maybe she acts all tough so people will notice her. Her mom and her stepdad basically ignore her. She told me."

"So what, you're Oprah now?" I ask.

Ella Wendy sighs and grabs my dish as I'm about to swipe off the extra salsa with my thumb.

"Think about it, Antsy Pants."

"WHAT? She told you? I'm gonna—"

"Get your tighty-whities out of your hiney," Ella Wendy says. "I'm far too mature for this elementary school drama. Cory told me your nickname when she was explaining things to me. That's all. She's not going to tag you with it in school anymore."

"You can't either," I say. "Or I'll start a rumor that you got expelled for smoking in the bathroom."

"You wouldn't! That would ruin my reputation!"

I wink. Ella Wendy relaxes. I help with the dishes, play some video games, then go up to my room to get ready for bed. **TICK, TOCK. TICK, TOCK.** It's 10:20 and four seconds, and Dad isn't home.

At eleven o'clock, I hear the barn door slide open and close. I climb down my ladder and find Dad and Ella Wendy laughing.

"What's the surprise?" I ask. "Is it—"

Dad cuts me off. "There you are, Anthony! Ella Wendy and I were just comparing notes."

At that second, Ms. Dreyer comes out of the bathroom.

Am I dreaming? Why is Ms. Dreyer here?

"Hello," she says. She's dressed in clothes much, much nicer than teacher clothes. Her high heels click across the floor, and she stands next to Dad.

I smile, halfway, at my teacher. "What's going on?"

"Ella Wendy," Dad says, "Why don't you make the introductions?"

Ella Wendy acts like a snake that's gobbled up a mouse whole. "Anthony. Dear, sweet, clueless Anthony . . ." She puts her hands on her hips, and goes into performance mode.

"Get to the point, Elwen."

"This is Crystal, my drama teacher," Ella Wendy explains. "And wait until you hear this! They have been dating. It's exactly as I suspected. I am a love genius."

KA-BOOM!

The room starts spinning.

I turn my eyelids into slits. "She can't be your drama teacher," I say to Ella Wendy. From the slits, I send out invisible darts and aim them at Dad. "She can't be your girlfriend."

"Sure, she can," Ella Wendy chimes in. She grins a toothy grin like the know-it-all she is. "Crystal is fabulous. I've been telling you about her, but you never listen!"

I stomp my foot like a two-year-old. "What? What the heck are you talking about? You don't get it, Ella Wendy! Crystal may be your drama teacher, but she's also Ms. Dreyer. Ms. Dreyer is my fifth-grade teacher! My teacher can't be my dad's girlfriend!"

Ella Wendy's mouth drops open. Then she screams, "OH! MY! GOSH! OMG! OMG!" She makes a mad dash for her phone. It'll take her a while, but by the end of the night, she'll have sent texts to everybody on the planet about what happened.

I yell, "DAD! You can't—"

"Calm down, son. It's not a terrible thing." He puts one arm around me, the other around Ms. Dreyer. Crystal. Whoever!

I breathe hard, but that doesn't take away the watermelon that's sitting on my chest. "If the kids at school find out, I'm toast! I don't need this!" I pound a fist on the couch and run up my loft ladder two rungs at a time. That's when I realize. Ms. Dreyer has just gotten a front row view of my pajama-ed butt. My teacher has seen me in my stupid baseball PJs! UGH!

Dad calls after me, "We'll discuss this tomorrow."

I turn to give Dad my dirtiest look. If I had a vaporizer, I'd vaporize him.

Ms. Dreyer doesn't say a word. Her forehead has wrinkles on it that I've never seen before.

In my room I slam myself into my beanbag chair and grab a pencil. I draw and draw and draw. I make myself into a mean and tough pirate. I give myself mean and tough pirate clothes—swords, boots, a black shirt, a big earring. I add a black vest, a couple of skull tattoos, and bulgy veins on ginormous muscles. My transport vaporizer is zoning in on Dad and Crystal, the lowly villagers I've captured. The vaporizer lifts them off my ship and drops them on a deserted island.

CHAPTER FIFTEEN
DEAL OR NO DEAL

There are a lot of things worse than having a dad who likes your teacher. Having your teacher see you in your pajamas is one. Having that teacher come to your place for Sunday dinner is another.

Dad and I had our talk earlier. He told me that Crystal promised she wouldn't let anyone find out she is dating a student's father. He reminded me that her job at Piperville Elementary was temporary. With a listen-up-I'm-your-father attitude, he adds, "Nothing you say or do will change anything. I'm seeing Crystal." And that was that. I listened up.

Ms. Dreyer and Dad are making dinner together. Well, Ms. Dreyer is making dinner. Dad is keeping her company. It's as if his lips and her cheek are magnetized and every few minutes they smack into each other. Yuck. The meatloaf is cooking, and well, it smells like a restaurant in this barn. Not a stinky restaurant, either.

I sink into the living room couch. I need to concentrate on mascot ideas. The only thing I've drawn so far is a talking meatloaf with two friends: a talking carrot; and a talking baked potato. Not good.

Ella Wendy dances in and flits around like a glittery butterfly. She's singing about elephants, but shuts up when the doorbell rings. She

runs to answer it then stops in front of the door. She turns and spreads her arms out like she's barricading it. "I have a surprise for you," she says to me.

"I've had enough surprises this weekend," I say. "Who's here?"

Ella Wendy slides open the door and yells, "Surprise!"

I'm sure the doc said I only need glasses for close-up work. But he's wrong. I'm not seeing straight. In front of me is Cory. But it's a different Cory than the girl I know from school. Or even the one I saw in my yard. This Cory is wearing a dress. A real dress!

KA-BOOM!

It's official. I hate surprises.

"C'mon in, Corinne," Ella Wendy says. "I'm so glad you could be here for dinner. I want you to meet Crystal. Oh, silly me! I forgot. You know her already! You're in Anthony's class."

Cory hasn't said a word. She frowns at me. I frown back.

"Excuse us, will you, Anthony?" Ella Wendy and Cory zip past me. I feel like my sneakers have been nailed to the floorboards.

Ella Wendy brings Cory into the kitchen. I hear Ella Wendy explain to Cory that her drama teacher, Crystal, and Ms. Dreyer are one and the same. That's why Ella Wendy wanted her to come to dinner. She wants Crystal to hear her sing. It's hard to hear what else they're saying, so I move closer.

Ms. Dreyer is talking now. "Let's eat first, all right, girls?"

Cory's not saying anything. I shouldn't care about why she is so quiet, but for some reason I do. Ella Wendy is yakking nonstop, as if she's had a couple of caffeine energy drinks. Cory slides away from the group.

I scramble to the couch and grab the drawing I was working on. I hope Cory doesn't talk to me. She's creeping me out tonight. It's the dress.

"You draw good." Cory is behind me, spying. "Are you entering that talking meatloaf in the contest?"

"Maybe," I say. "What's it to you?"

"It stinks like dog poo. I've seen some of your other drawings and they're not terrible. But this one is. Anyway, I know the best mascot, but I can't draw it," Cory says.

"No crayons?" I ask.

"Ha. Ha. You wanna hear it, or don't you, Ants . . . *Anthony?*"

"Not really, *Corinne*." Okay, so I do actually want to hear it.

Cory cringes at her name. "But first, I have a deal to make this time," she says. "If I tell you my idea, and you like it, and you draw it, and you enter it into the contest . . ."

"Keep going."

"Then you have to make sure I get to be a Piper Player and get a spot in the play."

"No way!" I shout. "It's our teacher who picks. Our teacher, a.k.a. my dad's girlfriend, the one who is in my kitchen at this very minute."

Cory ignores me. "Our school's mascot should be a carpenter ant. Get it? Carpenter Elementary? Carpenter ant? Ants are strong. They work together. They're cute."

I jam my fingers in my ears. "I'm not *listeningggg!*"

She yanks my hands away. "Eat that earwax, dork. And listen up.

Ella Wendy's gonna fix it so that Ms. Dreyer hears me singing tonight. You're gonna fix it so that she finds a spot for me in the play. Ms. Dreyer said it was too late, but you can find a way around that. Then you can use my idea and I won't sue your butt off for stealing it." Cory flips around and stalks off.

Carpenter ant? I find a clean page and start drawing. My hand whips around the page like it's on fast-forward. One ant, two ants, three ants later, I decide I don't just want Cory's idea. I need it! With it I have a chance of winning the mascot contest. Why do things have to be so complicated?

Right before everybody leaves, I hear *The Star-Spangled Banner*. The song makes me realize two things. One, Cory is obsessed about patriotic songs. And two, I need a plan.

After I give Cory enough time to get home, I pick up the phone and tap in her number slowly. "It's a deal," I say, and hang up.

CHAPTER SIXTEEN
THE PIPER PLAYERS PLUS TWO

For the last week, Cory hasn't called me Antsy Pants. Two other fifth-graders and two fourth-graders have. Plus a kindergartner, but she doesn't count. How can I completely ditch that name? How can I get a new one thing?

Swimming is for real athletes. Gymnastics is for real athletes. I am not a real athlete. What's left?

A couple days ago when I was flipping through the Insta-TV shows— the special shows you can order for $1.99, I did find something else interesting: music lessons. There was a guy on there who gave hour-long guitar lessons. I remember thinking how awesome it would be to be a rock star. That would be a one thing I could live with! I had doodled a bunch of photographers following me around with people begging for my autograph. When I came up for air, I remembered. I didn't own a guitar. I even checked in the pickup. No luck.

So, here I am in school today, thinking about my rock star dreams, and trying to listen to Ms. Dreyer. She acts like I'm no different from any other kid. This makes life easy for me. I have a hard time looking at her, though. Her lips have kissed Dad's. Yuck.

ANT

"Students," Ms. Dreyer says, "I have wonderful news."

Oh, no. I hold my breath. Please, please don't say you're my dad's girlfriend. Please, please, pl—

"Mrs. Merryweather is returning later this morning."

I let my lungs work again.

Lexie claps three times and then smiles an apology smile at Ms. Dreyer.

"She is speaking to Principal Paulson and will be here shortly," Ms. Dreyer says. "I'm just here to say good-bye."

Butthead Brad shouts, "Mrs. Hairyweather is back!"

Jordon Jerkenstein scratches both pits and lets loose a couple of ape sounds.

"Settle down," Ms. Dreyer says. "Despite certain challenges, I've enjoyed my time here at Carpenter Elementary. The superintendent has offered me a full-time position as the first grade teacher beginning next year. And although I won't see you because you'll be in middle school, I hope that you'll stop by and say hello."

"I'll come visit," Alicia shouts. "My little sister is in first grade."

"Next year, your sister will be a second-grader," Lexie reminds her. "She won't have Ms. Dreyer."

"Oh," Alicia says. "I'll come back, anyway."

Jillian giggles.

"Thank you, Alicia. I'll look forward to seeing you. Students, I also need to mention that mascot contest entries are due, not this Thursday, but next, so please get them in on time. And finally, Piperville's own community theater group, the Piper Players, will be performing in the community auditorium on Main Street that Thursday, as well as Friday. As some of you are already aware, I am the drama teacher. Please attend the show and support the arts."

Cory coughs a fake cough. *CAH! CAH!* It sounds like she's chucking up a hairball the size of a kitten. I get the message.

By the time math rolls around, Ms. Dreyer is history. Mrs. Merryweather is behind her desk, baton and all. I haven't missed her, especially her whiny voice. Today, it sounds like a cross between an Army drill sergeant's and a song that's been mixed electronically. At least I'll still hear Ms. Dreyer's milkshake voice. At home. Whether I want to or not. She's been at our place almost every night, playing chess with Dad, practicing play lines and songs with Ella Wendy, and cooking scrumptious dinners. For me?

In fact, Ms. Dreyer is at our barn when I get home from school. She's making the kitchen smell delicious again. My nose gets crazy-busy, and it sends signals to my stomach: *Alert! Alert! Brownies! Brownies!*

"Hey, Ms. Dreyer," I say, taking in a deep breath of yumminess.

Ms. Dreyer pulls two batches of brownies from the oven. "Now that I'm not your teacher anymore, can you call me Crystal? Please?"

"I guess I can. What are the brownies for . . . Crystal?" That was not easy to say. She is, and always will be, Ms. Dreyer.

"A bake sale. The money goes to the Piper Players."

I rock back on my heels and tip up on my toes. Is this a good time to ask her about Cory?

"I take it you want a sample?" Crystal asks. "You look hungry."

"That'd be great." I gobble up two brownies and try to talk. "Ms. Dwhreyer, Cwystal, I whanna ask—"

"Chew up, Ant," she says. She sounds more like a mom than a teacher. I chew, swallow, and grab the milk carton in the fridge. She stops me as I'm about to chug-a-lug it from the carton.

"Have a glass?" she asks.

I don't really want a glass, but I grab one anyway.

Crystal pours the milk for me, and I gulp it down. "I want to ask you something important," I say. "About Cory."

Crystal catches my arm before I wipe my mouth on my sleeve. She hands me a napkin. "Cory is a puzzle, isn't she? I about fell over when I heard her sing. Did you hear her? Unfortunately, she'll never get anywhere until she changes her language and her attitude. Nice to see Ella Wendy helping her."

I spit out what I want to say before I can't do it. "Can Cory be a Piper Player and be in the *Circus Follies?*"

Crystal tilts her chin. "Why? Why would you want her to be a Piper Player? I gather she's not a favorite classmate of yours."

I have a hard time lying, so I tell Crystal everything. Even about the mascot. She listens and nods, and puts her warm, brownie-smelling hands on my shoulder.

I plead again. "Can she be a Piper Player? Can she be in the show?"

"Auditions were weeks ago, Ant. Every part is taken. It's almost show time."

"There has to be something!"

"I don't know," Crystal says. She taps her forehead with her knuckles like she's organizing her thoughts. "Wait! There is something. I might be able to work this out."

"Awesome," I say. I reach for another brownie to celebrate.

"Don't worry," Crystal says. "I understand that Cory's had it in for you from the start of fifth grade, but is using her mascot idea going to solve anything between you two?"

"I can draw a great carpenter ant," I say. "It's better than any mascot I've come up with on my own."

A tiny sparkle comes into Crystal's eyes. "Well, since we're making deals, I want in."

What? Crystal is a dealmaker? I'm afraid I won't like Crystal's deal any more than I liked Cory's.

"If I find a part for Cory," Crystal says, "you have to do something for me. Come to play practice and help us finish the scenery. I'd do it myself, but I'm running out of time."

"You want me to draw and paint and stuff? You want me to be in the Piper Players?"

Crystal nods. "I saw your sketches a while ago when you went out for recess and left them on your desk. I got the opportunity to view your complete body of work. I have no doubt that you will— "

"My body of work?" I interrupt.

"Your doodles. Your sketches. Your drawings. What you create in your spare time. You're very talented, Ant. A little unfocused, maybe, but talented."

"I am?"

Crystal smiles. "Will you help us? Do we have a deal?"

"I don't have to sing, do I?"

"Only if you want to," Crystal adds.

"I shake my head. A humongous weight has been lifted off my shoulders. I'm not adding a new one. Even if I could sing. Which I can't.

Crystal explains that she'll have Cory sing *The Star-Spangled Banner* before the start of the play. "It's a perfect intro for what will come next," she says.

My DOODLES

Please doodle here if this is YOUR
copy of *Just One Thing!*

CHAPTER SEVENTEEN
ANT NEEDS A NAME

A couple of days ago at play practice, the dad of a Piper Player dropped off four ginormous walls with wheels on them. It's my job to paint a different scene on each. I like the job. It gives me something to do after school. The play is less than two weeks away. I have to paint fast.

Crystal walks by with a clipboard and a frown. Her frown changes to a grin once she sees the first wall I'm working on. "Nice!" she says.

"Um, thanks."

"I really like your use of primary colors against a black background. And the perspective you've chosen is intriguing. You are extremely good at this, Ant. You should be proud."

I look at the circus ring and the animals I painted. I tried to make it so that the audience would feel like they're part of that picture. I guess I did.

"Ant," she says, fidgeting a little, "I thought I'd take a ride into Philly this Saturday to the art museum. Would you like to go with me? Beforehand, maybe we could go past your old neighborhood. Your dad told me you used to live in South Philly. Might be fun to see it again."

"Sure," I say. "I'll ask if I can go."

Crystal smiles. "Your dad says it's fine."

More fidgeting. This time it's me.

"I'll pick you up about eleven o'clock." Crystal hurries off to get everybody together for the first run-through of the show.

Cory starts with the national anthem. Even though it's just dress rehearsal, Crystal makes us stop what we're doing, stand up, and put our hands over our hearts. Even the scouts who work the sound system and the spotlights have to salute. Once the show begins, everybody gets busy. Kids are saying lines and singing. There's dancing and prancing going on right smack in front of me. I hope some tutu-ed idiot doesn't pirouette into my paint tray.

As the circus ringleader, it's Ella Wendy's job to introduce each animal act by singing a solo. This makes my cousin beam brighter than the spotlights above her. The rest of the cast is made up of teenagers dressed like lions, tigers, bears, clowns, and ballerinas who perch on the shoulders of grown-ups dressed as horses. The show doesn't stink.

I'm painting faces. They're supposed to be the back half of the circus audience. I find Cory staring at me. She's about six feet away, offstage.

"You need brown and tan and yellow faces," she calls. "And put in some babies and parents, and a couple of old farts."

"Old farts?"

"Grannies and Grandpops."

I keep my paintbrush busy and don't look at Cory. "Why are you bothering me? You got what you wanted. You're in the play."

"Bite me," she says.

Her feet shuffle closer and closer.

"I don't have anything to do right now. I'm bored."

"So, go home."

"Crystal won't let me. How 'bout I paint?"

I look up and let out a huge I-don't-have-time-for-this sigh. Cory's dressed in a red, white, and blue flag jacket, and a blue skirt. It's wrinkled and looks like it came from the bottom of our laundry basket. She has on her usual black sneakers. I'm sure she thinks she looks patriotic, but she doesn't. She looks like a deflated Fourth of July balloon attached to a black clothespin base.

"Take a picture. It'll last longer," Cory spits out.

"Lens will break," I say, dabbing paint on a face a little too hard. I point to an empty wall. "I sketched a lion on that wall over there. You can paint that."

Cory quickly takes off her jacket and picks up a brush. I'm surprised she's pitching in. I won't tell her this, but I'm happy for the help. I'm also relieved she can paint inside the lines.

After practice, Dad and Ella Wendy and I head to the music store. He caught me watching the guitar channel yesterday and went berserk. In a good way. He said that I had to have a guitar. He was in a band when he was in college and played every Saturday night. If he hadn't smashed his guitar on stage during his last show, he would've given it to me.

I tell Dad, "I'm sure I can learn to play, especially if I take my time, and if I don't get bored with the TV guitar guy. Plus, I don't have to use my feet! I may even get good." Dad bites his lip. He's not convinced. Neither am I.

As soon as we get in the store, a man picks out a new shiny black acoustic guitar for me. Dad picks out a used brown scratched guitar that's on sale. Guess which one we get?

Ella Wendy is roaming around, grumbling. She's been in a bad mood since we got here. One minute she's a cheery ringleader, the next she's a grouchy teenager.

"I used to take piano lessons," she tells us. "At my house."

Dad puts his hand on Ella Wendy's shoulder and gives it a squeeze, "When your mom and dad are done with their tour, I'm sure you'll be able to take lessons again."

Ella Wendy plops down on the piano bench and runs a finger across the keys. "They don't think they'll be home for a long time, Uncle Jake. I suppose my voice is my instrument now. I can play it anywhere. But when I lived at my house . . . when I practiced the piano, it made Mom and Dad so happy." Ella Wendy puts ten fingers on the piano keys and plays a soft, sad tune. "I really, really miss them, Uncle Jake."

Ella Wendy stops playing. Huge, drippy tears have left splotches on her white ringleader shirt. I want to say something to make her feel better. A few sentences stick in my throat. (I'm sorry. I'll get you a tissue. Please don't cry. Please don't cry on my guitar.)

Dad saves the day. "Your parents are very proud of you," he says. "Don't you think so, Anthony?"

Oh, good, all I have to do is nod. I nod like a bobble-head doll. She can't help but notice.

And what do I get for it in return? Ella Wendy punches me in the arm! My guitar-playing arm. "OUCH!" I yell, even though it doesn't really hurt. This makes my cousin smirk, and I'm glad.

Once we finally get home, I'm too tired to try out any guitar lessons, so I decide to finish up my carpenter ant. I tack my poster to Dad's slanted desk and step back to take a look.

My ant is strong. He's happy, clean, and has zero zits. He's dressed in a green shirt and brown shorts and is wearing neon green Converses. I give him a tan baseball hat with a green four-leaf clover because I remembered that Mrs. Merryweather said the teachers used four-leaf clovers as eyes for their cartoon barn mascot. If any teachers are judges, I'm covered. I put a C on his hat and that can be for Carpenter. Or clover.

I take out the contest rules to make sure I've done everything.

Name? Uh, oh. What will I call him? Ant? Ha! Nope. No way. I settle on Carl because it starts with a C and he does have a C on his hat. Carl, the carpenter ant. I want to write his name on his shirt, but there's a problem. I want the letters to be . . . to be really special. Incredible. How can I make incredible letters? Then it hits me.

KA-BOOM!

I can use Ella Wendy's calligraphy set—the birthday gift that was supposed to be for me, but that I regifted to her!

"Ella Wendy," I yell. "Can I borrow your calligraphy set?"

"Why?" she asks, scooting down from her hayloft.

"I want Carl's name to stand out. He's the mascot I came up with. I mean, he's the mascot I'm drawing for the contest."

"Calligraphy is not easy, but I've been practicing. I can help, if you want."

"You can show me, but I have to do the letters myself. I don't want to get disqualified."

Ella Wendy writes "Carl" on a piece of scrap paper. Her hand glides over the letters and they turn out perfect. Then I do it. The letters aren't so perfect.

"Keep trying, moron," Ella Wendy says, grinning. "You've almost got it."

"Thanks, Elwen." I duck as Ella Wendy stands, but no punch lands on me.

Fifteen minutes later, after practicing Cs and As and Rs and Ls till my hand hurts, it's time to write

CARL

CARL on the poster board. I dip the skinny pen into the black ink and write the four letters without stopping. It's not bad. Calligraphy is kind of fun. Not as fun as drawing dragons, serpents, and other creatures. But still fun.

Let's see, what else do I need to do? I scan the rest of the list: Poster board. Check. School colors. Check. I check off the rest of the rules, then I see: Winner will be picked at the Halloween Social on October

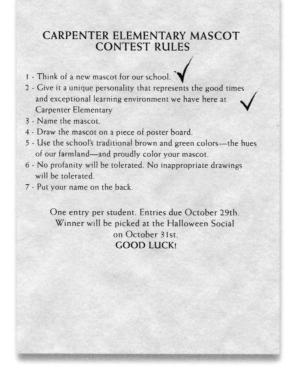

**CARPENTER ELEMENTARY MASCOT
CONTEST RULES**

1 - Think of a new mascot for our school.
2 - Give it a unique personality that represents the good times
    and exceptional learning environment we have here at
    Carpenter Elementary
3 - Name the mascot.
4 - Draw the mascot on a piece of poster board.
5 - Use the school's traditional brown and green colors—the hues
    of our farmland—and proudly color your mascot.
6 - No profanity will be tolerated. No inappropriate drawings
    will be tolerated.
7 - Put your name on the back.

One entry per student. Entries due October 29th.
Winner will be picked at the Halloween Social
on October 31st.
GOOD LUCK!

31. Oh, no! I've been so crazy-busy I almost forgot! Halloween! I need a costume! It has to be something scary, but not too scary. Our school has a rule about dressing up in costumes with bloody masks, rubber knives, chopped off heads, and fake blood. Anything that may make the little kids faint is off limits.

Somewhere Dad has saved my Halloween costumes. In the shed, maybe? Or one of the boxes piled up in the pickup? I can use my old Batman cape from third grade and be a vampire. Vampires aren't scary enough to break a school rule.

CHAPTER EIGHTEEN
CRYSTAL CLEAR

On Saturday, Crystal shows up at eleven o'clock exactly. Dad pecks her on the cheek, three times, like a rooster, and says, "You two have a great time in Philly."

Once in her mini electric car, we talk about the weather, the rules at Piperville Elementary, and the construction on the bridge that takes us over the Delaware River into Pennsylvania. But when the traffic gets bad, Crystal gets quiet. I can tell she wants to concentrate on her driving, so I put on my music, sit back, and doodle.

When we get into South Philly, I pull off my ear buds. "Yo, Crystal, I know my way around here. We're on Ninth Street, and my favorite place to eat is up ahead. I used to go there with my . . . um . . . I used to get sandwiches there a lot."

Crystal slides into a parking place next to Pat's King of Steaks. I can't believe it!

"I'm starving," she says. "How about lunch?"

"You don't have to ask me twice!" I say, and I dart out of the car to wait in line.

When it's my turn, I lean into the open window and shout out my order like a local pro, "One-wit-out!" You never forget how to speak Philly.

Crystal orders the same thing. "I have no idea what I'm about to eat," she explains, "but if it's good enough for you, it's good enough for me."

It's chilly and the wind is blowing hard, but we park ourselves on the benches outside, like everybody else. Crystal tells me about growing up on a lake in the middle of New York State.

"My cousin thinks you're a big shot from New York City," I tell her.

Crystal laughs. "All I offered up was that I was from New York. People like to assume things. I'm just an elementary school teacher who moonlights as a drama teacher. In fact, I love all the arts."

I chew on this for a whole minute and decide I've assumed some things lately, too. I've had Cory pegged only as a bully, and look how that's turned out. She's a pretty good singer, and she's trying hard to fit in with the Piper Players. Plus, she had that great carpenter ant idea for the mascot. There's a whole lot more to Cory than I ever would have guessed. I'm betting there's a whole lot more to Crystal, too.

After lunch, we ride down Ninth and pass the Italian Market. The fruit and veggie stands are still there, and I roll down the window to see if I can breathe in a garlicky smell. I wonder if Mama Matucci is cooking up some spaghetti gravy, and I get hungry all over again.

We weave in and out until I spy the William Penn statue, and I point it out to Crystal. For the next fifteen minutes, up until we get to the art museum, Crystal gives me a Philly history lesson. I could've done without that.

We park by the Rocky statue, and Crystal takes my picture. Then we charge up the steps, pumping our fists at the top like Rocky does in the movie. It's just what you do. Ask anyone from Philly.

I've run up those steps at least five times in my life, but I've never entered the big doors at the very top. Crystal motions me in and hands me a floor map. I can't believe that every inch of this place is filled with art!

Crystal and I wander through the hallways and in and out of the rooms. There are paintings and drawings and sculptures and pottery and freakish artwork I can't even explain. In one area, there's a tiny painting of colors scribbled in a circle. In another, there's a sculpture of an iron with tacks stuck in it. Crystal tells me that these works of art are priceless. She knows a ton about many different artists and how their work became popular.

"Art is art," she says. "If it has evoked an emotion in you, and you are confused, happy, sad, aggravated, or even indifferent, the artist has done his job."

I nod. I totally get it because I've felt every one of those things here today.

Crystal keeps going. "Your drawings do that."

"Do what?"

"They make people think."

"I am a doodler. I draw whatever I want most of the time."

"And most of the time, that's enough."

I think Crystal gave me a compliment, but I can't be sure. I slink away to study a metal ladder leaning at an odd angle against the wall. What does this artist want me to feel? Does he want me to study the angle of the ladder? The color? Its size? Is the artist saying something about stepping up in the world? Or climbing the corporate ladder? A guy in a janitor's uniform takes the ladder away. I am an idiot.

Crystal and I weave through more and more rooms. She stops often and quietly stares at things. I do the same. I decide I like what I've learned about art from visiting the museum. And if I've learned anything, it's that art can shut you up.

Before we find the highway that leads back to Jersey, Crystal drives down a side street. She pulls the car into an empty lot. Facing the lot is a humongous wall that's part of a row of brick warehouses. Someone has started painting children's faces on that wall. Each face is ginormous— bigger than Crystal's car. It will be a playground scene when done. And it'll take up a whole city block!

"Tell, me, Anthony, what's your opinion of this mural?" Crystal asks. "Any good?"

"It's really good. Who's the famous artist?"

Crystal's eyes light up. "No one famous. Just me."

KA-BOOM!

Crystal's one thing is that she's secretly a mural painter. And that is unbelievably cool.

Lately, I've had way too many surprises for a normal fifth-grader. Words are like peanut butter in my throat. I choke out, "You are the artist? Really?"

"Yes, me. Along with a group of artists I met when I moved here. I don't tell many people about it."

"Why not?"

"Everybody eventually finds something to call their own—a sport, a hobby, art. It's not always necessary that other people know what you do. You do it for yourself because it makes you happy."

CHAPTER NINETEEN
SHOW-STOPPER

There's a big box in Carpenter Elementary's main office. On the side it says:

MASCOT ENTRIES DUE TODAY, THURSDAY, OCTOBER 29th
WINNER ANNOUNCED SATURDAY EVENING , OCTOBER 31st,
AT THE HALLOWEEN SOCIAL.

This is it. I put my entry on top. Since the secretary is busy making coffee, I sneak a peek at the others. Jillian made a jack-o-lantern mascot; Lexie, a cowgirl (nice job, Lexie!); and Tyson did a . . . an ANT? It's a carpenter ant! WHAT? I quickly scan the others. There are four carpenter ants, plus mine. Cory sold me out! She gave that idea away to four other kids besides me. I bet she made a deal with each kid. When I see her, I'm going to punch her lights out. Okay, so I'd never do that but it feels good to think about it.

I'm so mad when I hit the sidewalk that I break out into a run to get rid of some steam. Inside our barn, Ella Wendy is pacing around in her loft repeating her lines. Every few lines she screams, "The show is tonight! I'm not ready! I'm not ready!"

"You're not the only one with problems, Elwen!" I shout up to her.

As I pass by the couch, I pick up a throw pillow and squish the living daylights out of it. I'm about to heave it up to the ceiling where I'm sure my **Cloud of Doom** is lurking, when Ella Wendy comes down the hayloft ladder. "Whatcha doing?" she asks.

I toss the pillow and turn off the TV. "It was a warm-up . . . for my guitar lesson," I stammer. "That's how I get the blood rushing to my fingers."

"Sure, moron. And I'm the Tooth Fairy." Ella Wendy collapses in a chair. "So play something on your guitar. I need a distraction. I've been running lines forever. It's stressful being a star, you know."

"Get. Over. Yourself," I say. I grab my guitar and play three chords.

"You've had this thing for a week and that's all you can do?"

"I'm pretty good, huh?"

"Ugh. No," Ella Wendy says, pacing around me. "Are you going to learn to play real songs?"

I put my guitar on the couch. "I've been busy with your play. But guitar playing may just turn out to be my one thing. If I can get better at it."

"Your what?"

"The one thing I can be known for by the time I get to middle school. The one thing that will not be Antsy Pants."

"Oh. That." Ella Wendy says, smirking. "Well, good luck, rock star."

I do some wild air guitar, and that sends Ella Wendy running for cover. Getting on Ella Wendy's nerves makes life totally interesting. It even makes me forget my troubles.

Later, we get ready to go to Ella Wendy's show. Dad, Ella Wendy, and Crystal are spinning around like toddlers who've overdosed on lollipops. Somehow, we manage to cram ourselves into Crystal's minicar. **TICK, TOCK. TICK, TOCK.** It's 5:32, and I'm about as antsy as ever. We're all a bundle of nervous energy.

Somebody has indigestion. *HICCUP!*

FAMILY PORTRAIT

ANT

Somebody else sighs. *Pshoo.*

Somebody farts. **FaRrrRT!** Oops, it was me. I had baked beans for dinner.

Ella Wendy's singing loud enough to wake the dead. *"Come with us to the circus. You'll see lions, and tigers, and bears. Come with us to the circus. And forget every one of your cares. Come with us to the circus. You'll see lions, and tigers, and bears . . ."*

Crystal's conducting from the front passenger seat. Twice she makes Dad swerve because her hands fly in front of his eyes. We almost take out a little old lady at the bus stop on Pine Street.

Dad is talking nonstop to whoever is on the other end of his hands-free gadget. "Oh, brother!" he yells. "Oh, brother!"

If I could zap myself to Mars, I would. Instead, I dig in my pocket for a pencil and sketch the beginning of a circus scene.

In the auditorium Crystal kisses Dad. On the mouth! She takes Ella Wendy's hand and together they run backstage. Dad and I find a seat in the front row. There's almost an hour wait, so I take out the picture I started in the car. I add a souped-up SUV with big tires. It's inside a circus tent and the animals are going wild. The SUV mows over a stunned elephant. The lion is freaking out because he thinks he's next. The zebras run and hide in the audience. Just like the ride here, Dad's the driver. He's wearing Nascar gear and mirrored aviator sunglasses. Crystal is the conductor, and I draw her pretty much as pretty as she is. Ella Wendy is leaning out the window, singing. I'm squished in the teeny backseat with my hands over my ears. My cowlicks stick up through the sunroof.

My drawing makes me giggle and a snort sneaks out my nose.

The music starts playing a mix of patriotic songs. That's Cory's cue to take her place and get ready to sing.

Crystal's voice comes across the loudspeaker. "Please stand for our national anthem." People shuffle out of their seats. "*The Star-Spangled Banner* will be sung this evening by Miss Corinne Joy Bennett."

Corinne Joy? Guess her parents goofed up her name, too. She must've been more of a joy when she couldn't talk. Cory struts to the center of the stage. Wait. Is that Cory? I can't be sure. Her hair is twisted into curls that sit on top of her head like a bird's nest. A very neat bird's nest. Birds would even perch there, it's so nice. She has blue junk on her eyelids and that makes her eyes electrified. Her red, white, and blue costume is the same, but the wrinkles have been ironed away. On her feet are fancy shoes with high heels like Ella Wendy wears to church. What the heck?

I'm so busy staring at her that I forget that she's actually doing the singing. When she finishes, after holding the last note for twenty seconds, everybody claps. Dad says, "Wow! Simply beautiful. Cory is very talented."

I'm about to fill him in on Cory's other so-called talents, like how she sold me out for the mascot contest, but he shushes me.

"Listen," he says.

Crystal's voice comes over the speaker again. "Ladies and gentlemen, please remain standing. Before we get to tonight's performance, the spectacular *Circus Follies*, I'd like a certain cast member to come out from backstage." The entire audience pays attention. "Ella Wendy Pantaloni, please step in front of the curtain."

I hear complaining and arguing. It's Ella Wendy. Her friends finally push her out from the split in the middle of the curtain. She saves herself from tripping at the last second and stands there, embarrassed. She's not sure what to do. I'm not sure what she should do either.

"This is weird," I whisper to Dad. "Nobody's practiced this."

"It's a surprise," Dad says. "Look over there." Dad points to the steps on the right-hand side of the stage. Two soldiers in full army gear walk up those steps toward Ella Wendy.

"It's Aunt Loretta and Uncle Ralph!" I say to Dad.

Dad winks.

"MOM! DAD!" Ella screams. She flies into their arms. They both pick her up and hug her so tight, I wonder if she'll break. Part of me knows Ella Wendy is thrilled to have this surprise. The other part wonders if she's going to punch them in their arms, like she does to me.

Over the loudspeaker I hear, "Welcome home, Captain Loretta Pantaloni and Lieutenant Ralph Pantaloni. Your daughter hoped you'd make it to our show. We are extremely honored and proud to have you here."

Everybody in the audience claps. The lady behind me blows her nose. Dad's tearing up. He keeps mumbling, "My brother. Oh, brother. Oh, brother!"

It takes awhile, but things calm down and the show goes on. Aunt Loretta and Uncle Ralph sit with us, and they stare at the stage and never look away once. Ella Wendy sings her heart out. It's like she's singing just for them.

No performer makes any huge mistakes. Nobody crashes into my scenery. The show is an hour long, and it goes by fast. The crowd goes insane when the curtain comes down for the final time. "*Whoo hoo!*"

At the end, Crystal comes on stage. Ella Wendy hands her roses and says, "The cast and crew would like to thank you for everything. Everything!" She blows kisses to her mom and dad.

There's more clapping, and then Crystal thanks the cast for their dedication and patience. She also thanks the tech crew and the parents. Then she says, "And a special thank you to our wonderful scenery designer, Anthony Pantaloni."

Blood rushes through my body like warm gravy. A kid who's working the lights points a blue spotlight on me. I'm purple.

Dad nudges me. "You're much better at art than swimming, gymnastics, or guitar, kiddo."

CHAPTER TWENTY

HOODWINKED ON HALLOWEEN

All of us go home to our barn after the play. Ella Wendy is like the wind, and it takes her five minutes to shove everything she owns into a duffel bag. She tosses it to Uncle Ralph and climbs down the ladder. "Good riddance, hayloft bedroom!" she shouts. Before she flies out the door, she turns.

KA-BOOM!

I get sucked into a surprise attack hug. Yuck. I don't hug back. Pantaloni men are not huggers. Instead, I pat her on each shoulder. Ella Wendy takes this as her cue to squeeze me tighter. To break us apart, I burp a deep, muscus-filled burp. BRrrRURP!

"Pig," Ella Wendy says, shoving me away. She shakes her head like I'm a lost cause and smiles. "Try to mature a little before I see you again."

"Later, Stinkygator," I tell her. It suddenly dawns on me that I shouldn't be calling my cousin these names anymore. She's always hated it—especially the Elwen one—and I never got why until this year. I smile and say politely, "Good-bye, Ella Wendy." I cough up a burp that sounds suspiciously like E**l**w**U**R**P**, but it happens by accident.

It takes until Saturday, but I finally admit (only to myself!) that I miss Ella Wendy. Dad does calculations for a new building. I attempt to learn a fourth chord on the guitar.

"You having any luck?" he asks.

I put down my guitar and stretch. "Nope," I answer. Then I say, "Are you?"

Dad chuckles. "No. It's too quiet. And I've got something on my mind. It concerns you." Dad tucks his pencil behind his ear and comes over to sit next to me on the couch.

"What?" I ask.

Dad spits out, "I want to spend more time with Crystal. Actually, I want her to spend more time with both of us."

I sort of saw this coming. "Oh," I say. What else can I say?

"Anthony, I realize we haven't known her for that long but you like her, don't you?"

"Sure, Crystal's great."

Dad doesn't wait for me to say more. He goes into a long speech about how he's not getting any younger, and how he loves Crystal. With a mess of worry on his face, he says, "This is hunky dory with you?"

"You mean you want Crystal to be your official girlfriend?"

"Something like that."

"What about Mom?" I hope I'm not whining.

Dad smiles. "Stay in touch with her, of course! And then he quickly adds, "Well, it's settled then." He pats my knee like I'm a two-year-old and goes back to his table. If he grins any harder, his cheeks will split.

I do like Crystal. Don't get me wrong. But we just got rid of Ella Wendy, and I was looking forward to it just being the two of us again. How much time will Crystal actually be spending here in our barn? I pick up my guitar again and strum a loud C chord. Dad's right. About two things: One, it is too quiet. And two, I am better at art than at guitar.

I put my guitar down and pick up my pencil.

"No more music?" Dad asks.

"We both know it'll be years before guitar is my one thing," I tell Dad.

Dad winks. "You worry too much."

The phone rings and Dad takes the call in the kitchen. I hear parts of the conversation. "Really? That good, huh? Mr. . . . I won't say . . . yes, we will be there. Good-bye." When he comes back into the livingroom again, he says, "Hey, I just remembered. Your school's Halloween Social is tonight. You're going, aren't you?"

"Sure. I wouldn't miss it! Dan Wharton, the famous artist, will be there. He's judging the mascot contest. Marcus, Lexie, and Jillian are coming by at six to go trick-or-treating for about an hour. When we get back, can you drop us off at school?"

"No problem," says Dad. "You'd better get ready. The pizza delivery guy's going to be here with dinner soon."

I climb up to my room and put on a black T-shirt, black pants, and the Batman cape. I load up my hair with Dad's disgusting hair gel and comb it straight back. This goop even makes my cowlick stick down! Ella Wendy left me some whitish make-up junk, so I smear that on my face. With red marker I draw a line of blood dripping out of my mouth. I hope I don't get a detention for that scary drip.

While I hang out waiting for my friends, I draw. I make a shadowy Halloween scene with a group (or is it a troupe?) of vampires. I'm the King of the Vampires, of course. My name is Vincento. Vincento may be the old guy at the market but his name sounds powerful, so I'm stealing it. It also sounds European. Transylvania's in Europe, right? I pronounce it Vin-chen-to because he has to have an accent. Vincento lives in a barn. Which makes sense because one, I live in a barn. And two, bats live in barns.

ANT

The doorbell rings, so I sweep my cape to the side and climb down
my ladder. Too bad I can't fly like a real vampire. Outside, Marcus is
dressed in a hockey jersey and he's carrying a hockey stick. He has on
a Freddie Krueger mask, but it's not the scariest mask I've ever seen.
"I'm sweatin' bullets in here," Marcus says. "Need ice."

We crack up.

Lexie has on a purple poufy skirt that matches her glasses, and a
silver sparkly top. Her wings are neon yellow.

"What are you?" I ask.

"I'm supposed to be a fairy," she tells me. "but they were out of fairy
costumes. My sister got this outfit together for me. It's made from her
old ballet costumes. The wings are leftover from my baby brother's
bumblebee Halloween costume last year. I am a mixed-up fairy. A fairy
failure. Is it awful?"

"It's nice," I say. "You look nice. I mean, your outfit is nice." You'd think an A+ student like me could come up with a better adjective.

Jillian is dressed in a Little Red Riding Hood costume.

Except that it's blue. "There were only blue capes left in the store," she says. "I'm a little blue about that." She giggles a very long giggle.

We crack up again.

As we head for the house next door, I spot a kid in a white sheet with cut-out holes for the eyes. As soon as the ghost barks out, "Trick-or-treat, smell my feet," I realize it's Cory. My arms get goosebumps. I am not in the mood for Cory trouble tonight. When she walks past, she knocks into me, on purpose. "Stupid, fake vampire teeth, dork," she says.

"Leave me alone, Cory," I snap.

Cory yanks off her ghost costume. "I'm not Cory anymore, remember? I'm *Corinne.*"

"Yo, *Corinne*, thanks a lot," I say, sarcastically. "Thanks for helping me out. Thought we had a deal. You're a traitor."

"What's going on?" Marcus asks.

"Nothing. It's between me and Corinne here."

Cory steps closer. "I wanted to give that mascot idea just to you, but I couldn't."

A creepy feeling is working its way up my spine.

Cory pulls my arm and whispers in my ear. "When I was over at your place for dinner and saw your talking meatloaf drawing, I knew you could draw better than anybody, and that you'd make the best carpenter ant. But Jordon and Brad found a paper where I had tried to draw it. And on that paper I put your name with a question mark. I didn't want them figuring out . . . that we're . . . um . . . friends, so I made sure a bunch of kids used the same idea." Then, with a mischievous grin, Cory adds, "Can't wait to dance with you at the social, Anthony." And she skips down the street.

"**Whoa!**" Marcus says, snickering. "You've got a new problem!"

The hair on the back of my neck stands up.

"Corinne likes you!" Lexie and Jillian shout at the same time.

KA-BOOM!

I'm dead meat.

CHAPTER TWENTY-ONE
THE THING

Once we get to the social, I spend every ounce of energy ducking in and out of kids, avoiding Cory. If I get within breathing distance, I think she might try to pull me onto the dance floor. I lean against the stacked gym mats and spy Brad Butthead and Jordon Jerkenstein sneaking extra cookies from an unguarded tray. Cory isn't hanging with them. I wonder if the Bully Squad fell apart when she became part of the Piper Players. Brad is dressed like a football player. It's easy to imagine him playing defense for the middle school team next year. Jordon's costume is a surprise. I thought Jordon would pick a tough-looking costume, but in her kitty costume she actually looks like a girl, for once.

Principal Paulson taps on the microphone. Everybody freezes. "I was extremely pleased with your enthusiasm over our mascot contest. Over sixty entries were submitted. The winners are as follows: Third place goes to Jordon Silverstein for a terrific drawing of a roadrunner."

Jordon shoves the rest of her cookie in her mouth. She prances to the front, grabs her ribbon, and meows.

There's another pop from the microphone. "Second place goes to Alexis Smucker for her colorful cowgirl mascot."

Lexie walks up to Principal Paulson, and corrects him. "It's *Lexie*, not Alexis."

"Oh, excuse me," the principal says. "I didn't realize. Congratulations, Lexie Smucker."

Lexie smiles brightly, thanks him, and returns to her place.

"Finally," Principal Paulson says, "Dan Wharton will present this trophy to our winner."

Mr. Wharton clears his throat and takes the mike. "I've judged a lot of contests, but this contest was unusual in that there were five ideas that incorporated the same theme."

No kidding!

"However, one poster did stand out more than the rest. Your new mascot is . . . drum roll, please . . ."

Zach lets loose on the drums—*BUM, deBUM, BUM!*

"A carpenter ant."

I can't look. This is torture.

Somebody is jabbing me with an elbow. I squint to my left, and it's Ella Wendy.

"What are you doing here?" I ask. "It's an elementary school social."

"Crystal picked me up. Dad's here, too. He stayed after he dropped you off. Open your eyes all the way, moron. Look at the poster Dan Wharton is holding up."

I turn. Mr. Wharton is waving my poster in front of the crowd. My knees buckle, and I feel the blood rush to my head.

"Anthony Pantaloni is our grand prize winner. It's his depiction of a carpenter ant that will grace Carpenter Elementary's halls for a very long time."

Hands clap. Somebody whistles. Somebody cheers. Kids point.

Am I dreaming?

Mr. Wharton continues. "Anthony has created a clever, unique, and meaningful mascot. His attention to detail in both the lettering and the mascot's body is beyond compare. With an eye for color, line, and dimension, this young man has captured the fun-loving atmosphere of Carpenter Elementary, yet the mascot is not portrayed as silly. I find the intelligent expression on the face especially intriguing. This piece is more than a poster of a school mascot. It is a work of art."

As Mr. Wharton stares at my ant, the crowd gets very quiet. Art museum quiet. People are looking at my poster, thinking about it.

Mr. Wharton snaps out of his trance. "Let's have another round of applause for this awesome artist."

Ella Wendy pushes me forward and starts chanting, "Awesome Artist, Awesome Artist." Kids, teachers, moms and dads join in.

I pick up my trophy and hardly remember thanking Mr. Wharton and Principal Paulson. When I walk away, people slap me on the back and say, "Congratulations!"

Dad and Crystal find me. Dad grabs my shoulders and says, "Proud of you, son." Crystal beams. I get the feeling she wants to hug me, but can't, because, well, if she does, she may lose her teacher job for next year. Either that or Dad has told her already that Pantaloni men are not huggers.

What a crazy night this has been! As we head out to the parking lot, I hear a fourth-grader I don't know say to his friend, "Hey, there goes the Awesome Artist. My brother will be in middle school with him next year."

Ella Wendy punches me. "Looks like you've got your one thing."

CARL

CHAPTER TWENTY-TWO
A PRESENT FOR ME

Dad has invited Crystal to Thanksgiving dinner, which means she's kind of like family.

KA-BOOM? Nope, no ka-boom. Not really. I'm okay with it.

Dad's been working overtime fixing up the barn. He even made sure there were bathroom doors up before our relatives started filing in. Nana and Pop Pop Pantaloni are here, and so are Aunt Loretta and Uncle Ralph, Ella Wendy, and a boatload of other people from South Philly who track me down to kiss me. Uncle Antonio, Dad's friend who is also my godfather, is here with his wife, Aunt Stella. If Aunt Stella pinches my cheek again, I may throw up on her fake leopard fur boots. I can blame it on the record-breaking amount of rigatoni I've eaten.

I'm not allowed to hide in my loft and draw, but I want to. Way too many huggers, if you ask me. For something to do, I bring my crickets in from the shed. Now that it's November and it's officially cold, they'll be better off living in the kitchen. Monkey Butt and Goo are alive and well. And so are the fifty relatives that live in their cricket cage with them. I wonder if *they* know all their relatives.

Nana comes in and squishes me in a tight hold for the second time. Either she can't remember she's hugged me already, or I'm irresistible. She reeks of perfume, and now I do, too. Good thing I love her.

"I hear you created a mascot for your school, young man," Nana says. "And lookie here!" Nana points a shaky finger to a framed pen and ink drawing. "This is a picture of you, isn't it? A self-portrait? It is so . . . so interesting. How creative of you to draw yourself sitting on top of the world. Speaks volumes, Anthony. Volumes."

Nana speaks Grandma, a language I've never understood. "I did that a few weeks ago," I tell her, trying to wriggle out of her super grip. "At art school in Philly. Crystal showed them some of my better

drawings, and now I take two classes there on Saturdays—intermediate drawing and cartooning."

"My grandson, the artist." Nana plants a lipsticked kiss on my forehead. "I will come to your first gallery exhibit called … ROACHES!" Nana screams. "*Mamma mia!* For gracious sakes! Pop, get in here! Bring the sprayer!"

"No, Pop Pop!" I yell. "These aren't roaches. They're harmless crickets. They're my pets. I must've left their screen door open."

My poor crickets are scared to death. And they should be, because Pop Pop—who didn't hear me—is aiming bug spray in their direction.

"Come here, you pesky pests," Pop Pop calls. "I'll git you."

"Nooo! Don't!" I dive for Pop Pop. I knock the sprayer out of his hands. Pop Pop gives up and shuffles off to the porch to finish smoking his smelly cigar.

I try to catch my crickets, but they're hopping everywhere! It's not easy catching these guys on a linoleum floor. I'm grabbing. They're running. I'm slipping. And falling! I'm not getting anywhere. What am I going to do?

All of sudden, I see an extra pair of hands helping me. Boy hands. Teenager hands. With a swipe, he scoops up a bunch of crickets and puts them in their cage.

"Spectacularly cool cage," the teen says.

"Thanks," I say. "Who are you?"

"Craig. Who are you?" he asks.

"I'm Ant."

"Yeah, I heard about you. You're Jake Pantaloni's kid, the artist. You rock, dude."

Just then Crystal and Dad walk in. "What do we have here?" Crystal asks, hands on her hips.

"I had to capture my crickets," I tell them. "This guy helped. His name is Craig."

"We've met," Crystal explains. "He's my son."

KA-BOOM!

Crystal's got a son? How many surprises can a kid take?

Dad and Crystal sit me down and explain that Craig is Crystal's son from Crystal's first marriage. He lives in California with his dad, but soon will be moving to Jersey. He's going to be a junior at Piperville High School.

I wonder if Craig knows what he's in for. Jersey's got to be a lot different from what he's used to. I can show him around. I'll especially show him what poison ivy looks like.

"I was about to get my guitar," Craig says. "And play some classic rock for the old geezer on the porch. You want to come?"

"I'll get my guitar!" I tell him. I don't even care that *Twinkle, Twinkle Little Star* and *Row, Row, Row Your Boat* are most likely not on Craig's playlist.

"Awesome, bro," Craig says.

Before I leave, something comes over me. I run to Dad and Crystal and give each one a hug. A split-second-no-one-will-notice hug. It hardly counts as a hug at all.

For Christmas this year, I'll still ask for that suspension bike, but I may not get it. I may get a stepmom and a stepbrother instead.

And I won't be regifting them to Ella Wendy anytime soon.

Nancy Viau

no longer worries about finding her one thing, for she now has quite a few things she loves, like being a mom, writing, traveling, and working as a librarian assistant. She is the author of the picture books *City Street Beat*, *Look What I Can Do!* and *Storm Song*, and an additional middle grade novel, *Samantha Hansen Has Rocks in Her Head*. Nancy grew up in the Philadelphia suburbs and lives in South Jersey.

Timothy Young

has done design work for *Pee-Wee's Playhouse*, the Muppets, Disney, *The Simpsons*, and Universal Studios. He is the author/illustrator of six published picture books including *I Hate Picture Books!* and *The Angry Little Puffin*. He lives with his family on Maryland's Eastern Shore.